STARKEEPER

Short Stories for Pilots, would-be Pilots and those interested in flying

JOHN L. HASH

The cover photo of a C-46 flying "over the Hump" in eastern India, was photographed by the United States Army Air Forces during World War II. It is in the public realm, but used with gratitude.

ISBN:0983168520
ISBN-13:9780983168522

For my parents:

John Wythe Hash

and

Beulah Grayce Lawler Hash

NOTE

Starkeeper is a work of fiction. Some of the events actually took place, but the characters involved are gratuitously inserted. Some of the characters are real persons. Considerable liberty has been taken by actually naming people in the book, and their indulgence is requested. In each story the Starkeeper is mentioned. The reader will quickly determine who that is.

1

NAGA CHIEF

This is a true story. Some of the characters' names have been changed.

****

"Which one of you is Dr. Hash?" The question was punctuated by a strong flashlight beam on the Captain.
"That's me," he said.
"The colonel would like to see you. Something urgent," he said.
"OK, tell him I'll be there as soon as I dress."
"Right, sir. Sorry to have awakened you."

*****

"Sorry to have awakened you, John."
"The sergeant said it was urgent," said John.
"Well, here it is. As you know, we have been trying for a long time to make friends with the Naga headhunters up on the border. The Japanese have driven them from their normal hunting grounds near here far up into the mountains. We received word just a short while ago that the Chief up there has a son who is heir

1

to his position as chief who has come down with some kind of malady. Reports are that he has high fever and has lapsed unconscious. You are the only doctor within fifty miles of this airport who has had smallpox. This may be what the boy has. I am asking you to take a native bearer and any medicine you think you might need and go to the airport, fly there with Captain Gallagher and do what you can for the boy. I am not ordering you to go, but I am asking on behalf of General Stillwell personally if you will consider it."

"You are right about the smallpox. The other doctors have teased me since I got here about that. I'll pack and be ready in an hour. Will the bearer meet us on the other end? How much can I take?"

"Take whatever you think you need. The bursar will issue you a thousand dollars worth of gold in case you need it to pay bearers or bribe someone to get where you are going. Your bearer will be armed and is one of them, so I wouldn't expect any trouble from his people, but there are lots of Japanese in the hills scattered about. Be careful. Come back when you decide to. We will get A.C. to take your patients while you are gone. If you need to brief him on your case load, please do so quickly. Time is short."

"Who will I be flying with?"

"Captain Gallagher is one of their most experienced hump pilots. His copilot's name is Goldwater. They have orders to accompany you, stay with you or their plane in their discretion and fly you out when you are ready."

"Wow! The Army Air Forces is going to spare two pilots and a C-46 for this?"

"You bet. Even Lord Mountbatten was briefed on your mission. He asked Stillwell to pick the team.

Stillwell called me. Good luck, John. By the way, don't tell anyone where you are going. No letters, etc. OK?"

"Sure."

"See you in an hour at the plane."

"Let's see, Atabrine, sulfa, penicillin, antiseptics, bandages, alcohol, water purification chemicals, surgical kit, anesthetics. Must be eighty pounds. Poor bearer," he thought.

It was nearly three A.M. when he met the Colonel at the airstrip.

"John this is Kevin Gallagher, Captain, United States Army Air Forces, and his Copilot Captain Barry Goldwater."

"Are you ready to go Dr. Hash?"

"Yes."

"General, thank you for your trust, we'll do our best."

"Try to radio me something if you can. My call sign will be Louis Pasteur. What call sign will you use."

"Mine will be Ralph White. He was my cardiology teacher in med school."

"Fair enough. Good luck. Come back soon and in one piece."

The big radial coughed and rumbled to life on the quiet tarmac. Even at three am, the temperature was over eighty five.

Chabua Tower gave them a green light to taxi to Runway 4. When the run-up was complete, Gallagher flashed his running lights once. The tower immediately responded with a steady green for takeoff authority.

As the RPMs came up on the big Curtiss Wright radials, the night lost all of its peacefulness. They urgently dragged the huge C-46 down the runway. Surely no one within a mile could sleep through that noise, thought Kevin as they raced down the runway. Into the night sky, they turned to a heading of three five zero and began the long cruise climb to twenty thousand feet.

Like Dr. Hash, Kevin had been awakened from a sound sleep. He and Barry had been called into the Major's quarters at the base. Like John, they were asked, not ordered, to go. After what General Stillwell had been through, he could have asked any one of the men for anything and they would have unhesitatingly given it. Joe Stillwell was the most inspiring kind of a person. The men adored him. He had suffered with them and come through one of the most brutal events of the war. Now, regaining his health with the eager assistance of the Medical Corps Hospital at Jorhat, he knew that these men were just as anxious to deal serious blows to the Japanese and drive them from this land.

"Twelve thousand, everybody on oxygen," said Kevin through the intercom. There were five airmen on board: the two pilots, a navigator and two airmen.

The moon shone on the snow-capped south slopes of the hump mountains as they approached.

"How long now to the airstrip?" asked Barry over the intercom.

"I make it just over an hour," Captain, said Lieutenant Brannon, the navigator.

"OK, thanks."

"How is the Doctor taking the ride, O'Malley?"

"Just fine, sir, he fell asleep on the climb out. Wish I could go to sleep like that."

"Let us know if you need anything, O'Malley."

"Yes, sir."

The only navigational aid in the area was directly behind them. As they flew away from it, the non-directional beacon at Chabua grew fainter and fainter.

Barry made his first celestial fix. "Good thing there's a moon tonight. I don't think we could find the field without it. How much runway do we have to land on, Kevin?"

"Four thousand six hundred feet. Turf. Said to be in good condition."

When Kevin compared the terrain's proximity below to the altimeter, he was impressed. The steep hillsides and gulches below were over eight thousand feet above sea level. He wondered if anyone had ever landed or taken off a C46 from such terrain. Moonlight shone on spots of ice and snow on the highest slopes. Steaming jungle below. July and snow, only on the roof of the world. What a craziness, halfway around the world from those he loved, more than a year since he had tasted his mother's pot roast; clothing that rotted before you could wear it out; leather turned green with lichen; jungle at the base, soaring rock piles to fly over to get cargo to China, ice on the wings in summertime, noisy planes painted dark olive drab, no fighter protection over China; overload cargoes; trucks cut in half and stuffed into the airplanes in pieces; drums of aviation gas lifted into C46's by elephants, no less; native bearers in wrapped pantaloons like the movies; the constant flow of material into China and wounded and sick coming out; record loads of passengers, Chinese, American, Australian, British, Malays, Nagas, Ghurkas, Sikhs, Hindus, Mohammedans; night flights over the hump, instrument landings at Chabua.....

"Hey Kevin, remember that B-24, Mr. Peanut, coming in on one engine? Lost three to ice over the hump and still made it to Chabua on one. Jamie said the old man put the entire crew in for the Air Medal for bringing the plane in. Just imagine two hundred miles on one engine descending at six hundred feet per minute. The crew said that they couldn't have made it another five miles."

"Something besides Bernoulli's principal holds these planes up, you know?"

"Yeah, I know," said Barry. There was a long period when neither said anything.

"Forty miles to the field, Kevin," said the navigator.

"Roger, thanks."

"What is the field elevation and runway number?"

"Field elevation is seven thousand three hundred sixty five. Runway 5 with the prevailing wind we have. How will we get this bird stopped in forty six hundred feet at that elevation?"

"Just hope the field is soggy. Guys have done it before, we'll just set up at ten above Vso (Stall speed with gear and flaps extended. Ed.) Many pilots refer to it as Stall speed with"stuff out." and plunk it on the threshold. Lightly loaded as we are, we have the best chance. Just imagine those guys bringing cargo or passengers up here!"

Morning twilight revealed the field. They flew a full circuit around it to get a look and then set up for an approach to runway five.

"Wake up the doctor, boys, we are about to land."

"He's awake and has been for a half hour."

Gear motors whined and flap actuators groaned. The big ship reconfigured itself for landing. Landing lights turned on only on short final approach to avoid being seen by Japanese.

Props full forward, manifold pressure to fifteen, flaps thirty, gear down and locked, over the fence.

The C-46 settled into the grass like a ballerina in "Swan Lake," transitioning from a flying object to a rolling object with deceptive grace. Big wingtip vortices swept up dusty clouds behind the wings as it settled onto its tail wheel. Kevin was on the brakes hard as soon as the mains touched. At eighty knots, that was a lot of metal to slow down before the far end of the field. The soft earth welcomed the C-46.

Kevin had plenty of room to turn around at the far end.

"Wow," he said to Barry, "I wouldn't have believed it if I hadn't done it."

"Nice landing," said Barry, stripping off his earphones and throat mic.

By the time they taxied back, post flighted and climbed out, the doctor was ready at the back door with his equipment. One of the crew swung one of the side doors open. There on the dusty ground stood a single man, dark brown complected, tall for a native, wearing light khaki trousers and a turban and a large silver ear ring.

"My name is Bumbi. I am your guide. How many will be coming?"

"How far is the village?" asked Kevin.

"About four kilometers," said Bumbi.

"We'll all go initially, except two of the crew will stay to guard the plane. Barry and I and Shannon will return here as soon as the situation seems OK. Don't you need more bearers to carry the loads?"

"Not this load. Besides, it's not a climb to the village from here."

"You speak such good English. How did you learn?"

"Methodist missionaries were here when I was a child. They taught all the village children to speak and read and write English."

"I would like to meet them," Kevin said.

"That is impossible now, they were taken by the Japanese and executed."

All of the Americans looked at each other. No one spoke.

"Take us to the chief, please," said Dr. Hash.

The village was located on a small almost level bench on the side of a long slope. Four to five hundred people lived there in tent like huts, mostly covered with animal hides and some canvas. The whole place had a very temporary look. Many of the villagers watched them arrive and followed them with their eyes. No one spoke to them until they stopped in front of one of the tents. A man of about fifty came out. He was dressed in a wraparound about his hips and wore a dark turban. He was lean and tanned. His gray beard and hair contrasted strongly with his dark glistening eyes.

Bumbi said to him, in English, "Sahib, I have brought the American doctor and the pilots who flew him here. His name is Dr. Hash."

"I am grateful to your people for sending you. My son is quite ill. Please come at once."

Dr. Hash followed the chief into his tent.

The boy was still comatose. His temperature was one hundred three. Pulse, one ten. He was sweating profusely. The chief said that he only awoke to vomit and urinate and had been like this for two days.

The red blotches on his face and body added to the other symptoms quickly confirmed that it was smallpox.

"Chief Ramad, your son has smallpox. He is very sick. If he is not treated, he will likely die. I have brought medicine from across the sea. I believe it will help him. May I give it to him?"

"If you and your chiefs believe in the medicine, so will I," said the chief.

"Please save him if you can. He will rule these people all his life after I make him chief, and I love him. My household is at your disposal. Let me or someone know of your needs. I am tired, now that you are here, I will sleep a little."

He put his leathery hand on the Doctor's shoulder in a gesture of thanks.

In about an hour, Dr. Hash came out of the tent. He went to Kevin and Barry.

"The boy is very sick. He has an advanced case of smallpox. If he caught it from any of the villagers, this place is a hazard. You both should return to the plane and wait there. I may be three or four days. I will send for you when I need you. Tell Louis Pasteur the situation."

"Do you think he will make it?"

"It is too close to call now. Maybe in eight hours I will be able to tell better. I will send a native to you this evening with a report. Stay clear of the village and all natives if you can. Eat and drink only what you brought. Do not bathe in the local streams, and take your Atabrine."

"Right. Good luck, John."

"Thanks," he said and turned back to the tent.

"Bumbi told me about smallpox," said the chief. "I will do what I can to prevent spread, but these people will be afraid and superstitious. They will believe me when I tell them that this sickness could kill us all. You are a brave man to come. Even if my son dies, I will never forget your kindness. I know my friend Joe sent you. Now I owe him my life twice."

All through the hot day, the boy's fever remained at one hundred three, plus or minus a degree. Dr. Hash knew that the sulpha would take effect quickly, but it had a hard fight on its hands. Smallpox had a strong grip on this young life.

Death and sickness seemed to be everywhere. Maybe it was just that the most densely populated countries in the world were at war and had been for several years. Several hundreds of thousands had already died. The Japanese had virtually subjugated China. They were everywhere, killing as they went. Millions were forced into labor to build the Japanese fortifications and runways.

On the allied side, the coolies labored also, but at least they were paid a small pittance for doing so, and they were working to be free. The long runway at Kunming was built by coolie labor. John remembered the huge stone roller pulled by hundreds of them to level the broken up rocks for the runway. That runway had cost half a million in gold, paid to Chaing Kai-Shek. Now the allied bombers pounded down its eight thousand feet and into the air of China to bring badly needed supplies to the fighting men and starving civilians. B-17s, B-24s, C-47s, C-46's, C-87s, C-54s by the hundreds landed, refueled, off loaded, reloaded and took off toward the hump. The Himalayas lay across the path to China. General Lewis had said that there was no such thing as weather here, decreeing that the planes would fly no matter what Mother Nature dealt out.

John remembered his wife and children. His older child was only four now. This young man was about eleven, just beginning to grow into a man. Would smallpox stop him now? John watched as the young man's chest heaved in rapid rhythm. Still no break in the fever. How much could this young body stand? If the fever went on for much longer, there was a good chance of permanent brain damage even if his life were spared. Years of preparation spread before him. High school, college, work, medical school, more work, more medical school, internship, then the war. He and his wife had been in their car on a Sunday morning, going to look at a house to buy in Nitro when the radio announced the Pearl Harbor attack. They turned around and went home. He called the realtor and told him that they were no longer interested. Surely there would be a war in the Pacific.

Pete and his other friends had gone to Europe earlier. Henry parachuted behind enemy lines during the Battle of the Bulge to set up an emergency hospital. He was awarded the Silver Star for that and deserved so much more. A country cannot give thanks enough for such unselfish heroism.

Now here John was at a station hospital in this steaming jungle. Steaming jungle? Not here on the side of the Himalayas at eight thousand feet. Here it frosted at night, but only two hours away, it was sea level and steaming.

The sun came up on a clear day. The day passed slowly. John stayed near the young man. His father came and went several times to check on him. John could see the hope dying in the father's eyes as the boy hovered. Sometimes, the boy would open his eyes and squeal softly and then fade back into sleep. No wonder smallpox is such an efficient killer, he thought. Just look at that chart. Fever of one hundred three degrees and no telling how long before I got here he had such a fever. The next four hours would be determinative. He would either begin to show signs that the sulpha was working and the fever would break, or he would convulse, become cyanotic and ultimately go into cardiac arrest.

"Starkeeper, come down and help this child. Help me. I am so alone. This smallpox has a strong hold on him. Several of the others are sick with it. An epidemic could wipe out this village. I am doing my best, but that is not enough without you. Help me Lord, you are my only hope."

Chief Ramad was standing next to him when John awoke. He was ashamed of himself for dozing off in the heat of the day. He had only slept six hours in the last two days. He instantly was fully awake.

"No change?" asked Chief Ramad.

"No change, still the high fever," said John.

"I have faith," said Chief Ramad. "I believe in your medicine. You must be a great man for Joe to send you."

"Any of us would have done the same for Joe, Chief. He is a very special man."

"You have sons?"

"Two. Younger than your son, across the sea with their mother."

At ten that night, the boy's eyes opened. His eyes showed surprise at the doctor's face so close to his, but he was too sick to move. John noticed that the sweating had subsided. He took his temperature. One hundred! The pulse rate was down to eighty five. Hooray. God bless the men who invented sulpha. This boy would live.

"Get the chief," John said to one of the women at the opening of the tent.

In less than a minute, Ramad appeared, fear covering his face.

"What is it Doctor? Is he dead?"

"No, chief, he will live. I believe the fever is broken."

The chief did not speak for a long time. His torso jerked as he fought back sobs. Finally he looked into John's eyes. Words failed him, but John knew what he was saying. They walked side by side into the tent where the sick boy lay. The chief put his head on the boy's chest and sobbed.

He stood, a bit unsteadily. "Thank you, thank you," he said.

"It was my privilege," said John.

In the morning, just after sunrise, the chief sent a man for John.

"Come with me," he said, "Chief Ramad would speak with you."

John went with him to a tent at the end of the row.

Inside, in the growing light, Chief Ramad handed John a rolled up animal skin.

"This is a snow leopard skin," he said.

"These animals are revered by us and are not killed except in self defense. I have nothing of greater value. I and my people will forever be in debt to you and your people. Take this to remember that you saved a young chieftain for us. Thank you so much."

John gently took the pelt and held if reverently.

He said to the chief, "I will tell your friend Joe that I was welcomed here and that you and your people are his loyal friends. It will be more precious to him than any present."

"You and your friends will go now?"

"Yes, Bumbi and the women can see to giving your son the rest of the medicine. He will recover completely, but it will be several days before he will want solid food. Feed him soup and liquids until he asks for solid food. I must go before my people catch smallpox. May I leave you now?"

"Go, and take our gratitude with you to your people. We will never forget you."

"Thank you, Chief Ramad, it was an honor to meet you."

At the airfield, Kevin and Barry were glad but surprised to see John, walking in with Bumbi.

"The boy will live. Let's go home," John said. They quickly prepared and boarded the waiting C-46.

The rumble became a roar, and the roar a great snarl as the C-46 ran up to full power before Kevin and Barry released the brakes. Huge swirls of dust billowed up behind the wings. Then, at release, the huge plane lunged forward. In six hundred feet, the tail wheel lifted. Long down the runway, it lifted into the hot day, turned slightly and climbed into the sunlight.

2

THE PM

"Kevin, Barry, Joe radioed personally to thank you and John for going up to Naga country on that medical mission. Personal bonds mean a lot in wartime. Joe was especially grateful. You will hear more about that later directly from him."

"What I have for you now is top secret. As of now, you are to discuss this mission with no one. Do not discuss it among yourselves except when you are sure you are alone."

"What is it Colonel?"

"A passenger trip. Night flight. No fighter escort. Over the hump to Mongolia."

"Mongolia, that's a thousand miles," said Barry.

"Right," said the Colonel.

"You will leave here at dusk and fly at night to a remote airstrip in Mongolia. A crisis has erupted concerning our Russian allies. Seems that they will not give our merchant marine the charts they need to navigate into the Arctic ports to bring in supplies and war material. They are so afraid to give up any information that this must be talked out at the highest levels. Your passenger and his group will arrive at Chabua this afternoon. They will rest and brief Lord Mountbatten here. Since the British Air Forces have no ongoing activity in this part of the theater, he insists that our experienced pilots fly this group to Mongolia, wait for them as long as it takes, and bring them back or take them wherever they want you to take them. Officially, you will be detached to them as you take off here. Kevin, you will be in command of the Americans on the trip, but you will take orders from a British Group Captain named Bannister."

"How many souls?" asked Kevin.

"Maybe eight," said the Colonel. "OK, get some rest. Is your ship fit?"

"Yes, sir, it is," said Kevin. "Those Curtis Wright engines were just overhauled less than four hundred hours ago. The airframe check is current and there are no squawks that I know of."

"Since your plane is fitted with long range tanks, you were logical candidates, besides Joe asked for you. This will be a maximum range flight. No fuel stops are planned. Fuel for the return trip is being brought in by yak train. You are to maintain radio silence once you depart Chabua. Overfly the destination field on approach. You will be given a light signal to land. If no signal appears, fly on to the alternate, some fifty miles further and land. There will be provision for a few light arms on board, but, as you know, weight is critical."

"Who is the head man on the trip," Colonel?

"I will tell you that right before departure. All this is on a need to know basis. Get some rest. Say nothing to anyone."

"Yes, sir," they said in unison, saluted and left the Colonel's office.

They gave each other that look as they walked back to their tent. They packed a light bag each, cleaned and oiled their sidearms, drew rations at the commissary and returned to the tent to await their summons.

When they knew they were alone, they got out the chart that the Colonel's sergeant had given them. It was well marked with elevations, visual check points and distances. The compass deviations on the trip varied by ten degrees. For one thing, they would pretty much be in one time zone, though.

They visited the met office to get a weather briefing. The Major in charge took them into his private office for the briefing, since the trip and destination were secret.

"I don't see any real difficulties with the weather. There is a large high pressure dome over central Asia and this time of the year, there is always the threat of afternoon thunderstorms, but there are no fast moving fronts, no monsoons or cyclones, so it shouldn't be too bad. No way to tell now what the weather will be like for your flight back. Just keep an eye peeled for the weather while you wait. You can tell a lot about what is coming by what you have, remember."

Nothing seemed out of the ordinary. Having a Lancaster land at Chabua was not a rarity. Cars were taken out to the planes which stopped on the taxiway at the remotest part of the base. The cars then went to the Officers Club where Kevin and Barry had been ordered to report when summoned. Late in the afternoon, a corporal came to their tent and told them that their Colonel wanted them. They hefted their bags and walked in the scorching sunlight over to the Officers Club.

The steward at the door directed them up stairs to the Senior Officers Mess. In the hall outside the doors to the Senior Officers Mess were two British MPs. As Kevin and Barry approached, they snapped to attention.

"Captains Gallagher and Goldwater to see Colonel Harris," Kevin said.

"One moment, sirs," said the shorter man. He disappeared inside without making a sound with the door. In a moment he was back and said, "Step inside, sirs."

Inside the large room were two parallel tables covered with white table cloths. At one table were several men dressed as civilians. The other table was surrounded by officers he recognized and some he didn't.

"These are your pilots, gentlemen," said the Colonel motioning Kevin and Barry to stand easy. A tall but stooped figure in mussed U.S. Army dress stepped out of the group. He approached, hand held out.

"Thank you both for that trip to Naga land. Ramad is a strong ally and a good friend."

"You are welcome, sir, we were honored to be involved."

Good Lord, meeting General Joe Stillwell in person!

"Come sit with us. Hope you don't mind not dining with your comrades."

They stepped forward and sat at the table. From their side of the table they could see across to the second table where the men in civilian clothes sat. At the right end was Louis, Lord Mountbatten himself. Holy cow!

The door opened again. In stepped Major Hash. General Stillwell rose to greet him, too.

"Major Hash, good to see you again. Your grace, Major Hash is here."

With that, Lord Mountbatten rose, retrieved a paper from an aide and approached.

"Your grace, may I present Major John Wythe Hash of the United States Army Medical Corps, Captains Kevin G. Gallagher and Barry R. Goldwater of the United States Army Air Forces."

"At ease, gentlemen." Turning back to address the men at his table, Lord Mountbatten said, "If you will give me your attention for a moment, please."

"For those of you who don't know, these are the three officers I mentioned earlier. With your indulgence, I would like to read this to those assembled."

"Attention," said General Stillwell. All officers and others rose to their feet.

"On behalf of King George, V, and with the thanks of a grateful nation, for bravery above and beyond the call of duty, these three men, Major John Wythe Hash of the United States Army Medical Corps, and Captains Kevin G. Gallagher and Barry R. Goldwater of the United States Army Air Forces, flew at night over the Himalaya mountains to a remote airstrip to tend to a smallpox victim who is the son of a leader of an ally of Great Britain and the United States. At great risk to themselves, then they subjected themselves to the risk of contracting smallpox to tend to the sick child, and ultimately, with the assistance of modem medicines, saved the child's life and those who would have doubtless been infected by him. Since the subject child will succeed to leadership of his people, the feat is deemed to have been the equivalent to saving the life of the head of a state. Therefore each of you is hereby awarded His Majesty's Victoria Cross with Air Medal for Bravery, and the thanks of all of those who love liberty. God save the King."

There was a long silence, then a polite but thorough round of applause.

Then a squat man, with a big cigar in his mouth said.

"Enough already, Louis. You have doubtless startled these good men out of their appetite. Quit the prattle and get back over here, and bring them with you. I want to shake their hands." With that Lord Mountbatten led the men over to the other table to shake the hand of the outspoken gentleman.

"So you are the pilots who are to fly us up north? Good to have you, gentlemen. Now get yourselves a good lunch. I daresay that it will be the best meal you will have for the next week or so. And you, Dr. Hash, will you do us the honor of staying for lunch? I would very much like to have my picture made with all three of you afterwards."

It was a good meal, but each of them had a hard time swallowing for a while.

The heat of the day had not even begun to give up when they gathered beside the C-46 a half an hour after sunset. Eight men, all dressed in civilian clothes, boarded. Kevin and Barry did a very careful weight and balance. They didn't often carry near this much fuel. The hop over the hump was not that long and every pound of useful load that could be dedicated to cargo, was. Now this night, the cargo was eight passengers and luggage, probably one twentieth of the load they could carry with a light fuel load. But tonight, with all of the reserve tanks filled to the absolute maximum, dripping fuel as it expanded in the hot tanks after being cool underground, the plane was to carry a different kind of load aloft. Two men stood by with fire extinguishers as they cranked engine number one. Like a good soldier, it started correctly, belching a great cloud of blue oil smoke and then settled into an irregular rumble in its cowling. Number two came up just as obediently. You didn't have to wait long for the oil temperature to come up into the green range on the gauge here in Assam. As soon as the tires could be seen rolling, the two men with fire extinguishers put them down, saluted, then picked them up again and retreated to the waiting van.

Wow. A night takeoff with a full load of fuel and those particular souls aboard. Every item on the checklist was checked and double checked. Kevin and Barry had each separately walked around the C-46 and checked everything. The ship was fit, alright, but this trip was so important, they took their sweet time checking everything. Now it all came together. The run-up on each engine was smooth. Not even a burble or cough as they checked the magnetos.

"Ready to go?" Kevin asked.

"Ready here," said Barry.

"Give the tower the lights."

Then they saw a steady green light from the tower. Kevin pushed the two big throttle levers forward slowly. He was always amazed at what happened when he did that. Outside on each wing, the rumbling radials awoke, grumbling at first, then bellowing, then roaring, then snarling, then screaming as those big propellers reached full revolutions and full manifold pressure arrived. Tonight, he eased the throttles forward, walking them up to their stops deliberately but not quickly. The C-46 heaved forward, smoothly gaining speed. The tail wheel came up, Kevin put on a little backpressure and, after a few seconds, it lifted easily into the twilight.

"Positive rate of climb, gear up," he called.

"Gear coming up," responded Barry.

"Climb power," said Kevin.

"Back to two thousand and thirty six inches," said Barry.

Tonight this was probably the most important airplane aloft in the world. In the passenger compartment were two, at least, of the most important people in the world. The C-46 smoothly cruise-climbed through five thousand on its way to fifteen thousand. The last red glow in the west faded into indigo. Inside the cockpit, the glow of gauges was the only light. Twelve hundred miles, navigating by the non-directional beacon behind them at first, then by the stars, and at dawn and daylight by visual check points on the ground.

"Go, baby, go" Kevin thought.

"Here we come. We are yours for another night, Starkeeper."

"I'm going to go back and brief the passengers, Barry. You take it."

"OK, I've got it."

Kevin went back through the red lighted cabin. Due to the noise, he had to almost shout to be heard. He told them that soon the temperature would begin to drop dramatically, that they should don the fur lined suits for comfort and that when the light flashed, they would be climbing through twelve thousand feet and everyone would need to go onto oxygen. He showed them how to don the masks to receive oxygen. He also told them that they could sleep with the masks in place if they wanted to. If they needed anything, either press the button on the side of the cabin or send someone forward. The hastily assembled and installed seats were not the most comfortable, he knew. He offered cotton balls for ear plugs or regulation ear plugs for those who could stand them.

"We will be cruising at twenty thousand gentlemen. I expect a smooth ride, but I would advise and request that while seated you keep your seat belts fastened. Later if you get hungry, the crew chief has hot coffee in thermos bottles, doughnuts, or as you call them, crullers, I believe, and sandwiches. Have a nice flight and let us know if you need anything."

"Thanks, Captain," said the older man with the unlit cigar clenched in his teeth.

"They seem OK back there, no complaints," he said.

"What good would it do for them to complain," asked Barry, "the PM would probably make them jump." He smiled.

"That really is him back there, isn't it?" Kevin asked.

They could see now over the peaks of the Himalayas, On the north sides of the peaks were great smooth layers of clouds obscuring the terrain below.

"I hope that clears before too long, once we get close, we will need ground contact to find the field. Star fixes are not that accurate."

"How much time on those outboard tanks?"

"We ought to change in ten minutes," said Barry.

As the flight droned on, everyone seemed to settle in. The C-46 rumbled along through the night, "Hey, Kevin, that right outboard tank isn't feeding," said Barry.

"Try the switch again, Barry."

"OK."

Ten minutes later, "Still not feeding from the starboard outboard, left's OK though."

"Go back to the right main while we try to figure this out. Time now is 2314."

"We really need that fuel," said Barry.

"I know if we can't access that tank, we are in for a long night of cross feeding and the probability that we will not make our destination. Where the hell would we divert to if we needed to? Most of this area on the ONC chart is marked uncharted."

"I've tried several times to get the electric valve to open, do you have any ideas?" asked Barry.

"The only other time I have seen this was when I was co-pilot for Wade Hampton when I first got here. He tried rocking the aircraft and got the valve unstuck that way. Before we try that, I should tell our passengers. If they are asleep, the upset could alarm them."

"Why don't we wait and use the other tanks, I would not try any maneuvers in the dark, especially over such high and hostile terrain. Let's stick with the right main for the next two hours, then take another look."

"Anything on the ADF?"

"Maybe Tokyo Rose has some interesting stuff tonight. That is one station you can always count on. The Japs bust their butts to keep that transmitter on the air. Lots of power, too."

"...our program. You American boys should know better than to try to take Guadalcanal. Don't you know that the best soldiers in the Japanese Army are defending Guadalcanal? You will surely fail and a lot of you will die trying. Why don't you prevail on your leaders to forget this foolishness? Try some nice easy little island this time, you know you are not ready." Then we heard her say, "Especially for you boys in the Submarine Command in the Malacca straits, here is the latest hit by the Andrew Sisters, 'It's Been a Long, Long Time.'"

"You know what really bothers me about her is that she is an American. If she were pure Japanese, I could stomach it better, but just think, she has been one of us for a long time, and now this."

"Yeah, it stinks."

"You know, if we keep that off the right wing tip, and adjust a degree every hour or so, we should be able to at least track a roughly north course line," said Barry.

"I make it about an eight degree crab to the left to maintain a northerly course, don't you," Kevin said.

"Yeah, eight is right," said Barry.

"We are starting to pick up a little ice now."

"We sure could do without the Himalayan hospitality tonight. It's only light rime now, but we'll keep a sharp eye peeled."

Light icing came and went a dozen times through the night.

"Looks like time to shake that outboard," said Barry as the sun began to lighten the eastern sky, "I'll go this time and brief them. What if they won't let us maneuver?"

"I'll tell them to prepare for a yak ride if and only if we can find a suitable field short of our destination. This is serious, Barry, and I know you know that. I'll try to impress them that we really need to shake this valve open and that we may maneuver rather drastically according to their standards," he said and squirmed out between the seats and throttle quadrant.

At five in the morning, with the highest of the mountains behind them, Kevin decided it was time to brief the passengers on the fuel valve problem. He left Barry at the controls and walked back into the cargo bay, now passenger compartment, of the C-46.

"Gentlemen, I need your attention for a minute." Those sleeping roused or were roused by the others.

"We have a problem with one of our fuel valves. It is on the outboard tank in the starboard wing. The valve is controlled by an electric switch and has not functioned since we departed Chabua. We have tried all night to get it to function, to no avail. That tank contains two hours of fuel. We absolutely need one hour of that fuel to get to our destination. We have been cross feeding fuel overnight because we did not want to maneuver over the mountains. I had this problem occur once on a similar aircraft when I was a copilot two years ago. We were able to get the valve to open by rocking the aircraft and repeatedly toggling the switch in the cockpit. I would like to try the same thing now, but I wanted to tell you about it beforehand, does anyone have a question about our plans?"

"Captain," said the PM, "Do what you think best. We are in your charge and we want you to do what you can to get us to our meeting."

"Thank you, sir. I will flash the red light above you twice before we start to maneuver. I will flash it again twice when we have finished maneuvering."

When he got to the cockpit, he asked Barry, "What do you make our altitude above ground level?"

"When I can get a glimpse between clouds, it looks like high plains below us now. I estimate ground level at about six thousand MSL. That gives us fourteen thousand feet above ground. What sort of maneuver worked for you before?"

"Gentle rocking to slosh fuel against the valve body first, and gradually getting more bank until it worked."

"What angle was necessary before?"

"About fifty degrees."

"How about if I watch the altimeter carefully while you concentrate on the rocking?"

""Good idea. I expect we will lose up to one thousand feet if we get into a fifty degree bank. Watch the airspeed carefully too, Barry. The plane will accelerate rapidly in descent."

"OK."

"Here we go."

With that he began to rock the big cargo plane, gently at first. A twenty degree bank repeated from side to side was not enough. Only lost minimal altitude with that. Next, he tried a thirty degree bank and held it with the right wing up for a whole minute. No go, and thirty degrees cost them fifteen hundred feet, No problem with that, but repetitions would eat into the rest of their altitude above ground level.

Now he was rocking the ship from right bank to left bank at forty five degrees. That ought to work, he thought. But it didn't. At the maximum right bank now, he turned the yoke full over to the left and held it. The big plane began its roll to the left, now twenty degrees right wing down, now level, now ten degrees left wing, down, still he held the yoke full over. Now twenty degrees, thirty, forty, fifty, sixty, then he let up and returned the big plane to level. That cost another two thousand feet.

"Still no go, Kevin. That thing sure is stubborn. If we can't shake it loose pretty soon, we need to begin to look for an alternate."

"I agree. Let's give it one more try."

"OK."

Now starting from wings level, he heaved the yoke over to the left. The big airship banked, ten degrees, twenty, thirty, forty. He added some right rudder, now more right rudder, now full right rudder and still he held the yoke over. Sixty degrees, seventy degrees, eighty degrees. The airspeed showed near Never Exceed Speed. The altimeter was unwinding so fast he could catch its sweep out of his peripheral vision. Still lie held it over. Now ninety degrees, full right rudder. Now at "never exceed speed." Quickly he reversed the yoke to full right. The great freighter reared toward the right. The airspeed began to come back to normal. The altimeter slowed its unwinding. Things began to quiet down. The vertical speed indicator indicated a beginning of a return to level flight. Neither man spoke for a couple of minutes. Barry reached over and toggled the red lighted switch twice.

Then after a couple of minutes as they focused on it, the number two outboard fuel gauge began to rock, indicating that fuel was flowing from the outboard tank into the next inboard tank. Now it could be fed to any engine through the cross feed system as need be.

"Whew," said Barry.

"Now we have enough to go all the way. Good thing, too. That ground below, while basically level is hostile looking, lots of little gullies and big rocks."

"I'll be right back," said Kevin, and wriggled out of his seat to walk back.

"Gentlemen, thank you for putting up with our aerobatics. We were successful. We now have sufficient fuel where it can be cross fed to complete the flight as planned. Now that dawn is approaching, we will determine our exact position and navigate to the rendezvous field."

"Good, now we can make it," he thought.

"Long night, huh?"

After the big Wright engines had pulled them through most of the night, the edge of the blackness to their right began to turn to blue. In less than half an hour, the C46 was in sunlight, still seeking its objective.

"Kevin, we'd better find a clear spot soon, or we have got another little dilemma," said Barry.

"It's been under cast for hours, I sure hope we can find a hole before we get there."

"By the way, how do you plan to establish when to begin your descent?" asked Barry.

"We don't have anything more precise than a star shot and Radio Tokyo at five o'clock off our right wing," said Kevin.

"Let's get a look at the ONC chart in the area of our destination and see if we can make a list of ground check points to look for."

"According to the chart, this airfield is just north of an area of uncharted desert."

"We may have to overfly a bit and locate ourselves and come back."

"According to the chart, there is a dry river bed that runs perpendicular to the landing field. If we can locate the river, we can go up and down to look for the field."

"There is a small hill about five miles east of the field. It seems to be the only break in the consistent elevation within several miles."

"Here we are, VIP's in back, no navaids on the ground, no fighter protection, probably five hundred miles from any other aircraft aloft, over a solid deck of clouds, fuel supply less than one and a half hours, uncharted terrain below, ah, the joys of air travel."

"We are still at twelve thousand, maybe if we dropped down closer to the cloud deck, we could duck under if we spot a hole."

They set up a gradual descent by pulling back the power to twenty five inches of manifold pressure. The big C-46 began to descend at five hundred feet a minute, solid as a rock.

"No turbulence at all, is there?"

"Sure is smooth, great for our passengers' comfort."

"By my reckoning, we should be about fifty miles short of the field. I am assuming that the winds aloft didn't change much since midnight."

"Isn't that a hole over to the left?" asked Barry.

"Sure enough, let's go look."

With that he heeled the C-46 over into a thirty degree bank.

When they got closer, they could see that the hole was actually the top of a flat hill, projecting just to the top of the cloud deck. Could that be the hill on the chart?

"I believe that I saw a river through the break just as we got to the right angle from the hill," Barry said.

"If that's correct, then we made better time than I thought. We are fifty miles further than I calculated. If that is our hill, then the field is about five miles over there to the right," he said, as they began a shallow right turn.

"I can see the ground over here, Kevin. There is probably three thousand feet below the cloud deck to ground level. Let's drop down and look for the field."

Just as the deck passed in front of the nose, they both spotted a group of dark vehicles parked in a line on the tan colored sandy terrain.

"What luck, there's the field," Kevin said. "Tell the passengers while I circle that we are about to land."

"OK."

When Barry got back, Kevin had the pre-landing checklist at the ready.

"Power back to eighteen inches, gear coming down."

"Two green for the gear, flaps coming down to ten."

On downwind, they got their first look at the field. Seven or eight vehicles waited below. They could see a group of about thirty men.

"No tanks, no armored cars or other hostile stuff," said Kevin.

"Let's land to the south."

The C-46 smoothly turned left to begin the squared "U" turn that pilots call a pattern. Unnecessarily, Kevin turned the landing lights on when they swung around to final.

The field was well groomed and the sand slowed them as they rolled out, Great billows of dust followed them back to the cars where they shut down.

After securing the cockpit, they went back to see to their passengers.

"Captain Gallagher, thanks for getting us here. We all know it was not an easy trip for you."

"Actually, we were very lucky locating the field, sir. How do you want this to go, sir?"

"If you and Barry can stand it, we want you to stay with the plane. Our group will go with our hosts to a nearby compound of buildings and do what we came for."

"If we need you, we will summon you. If you need us, one of you come get us. I am given to understand it is less than a mile."

The passengers climbed stiffly down the steep ladder. Kevin and Barry watched from the cargo bay. The tall British Army Group Captain went first, then he turned and introduced each member of his party to the hosts.

"My gosh, that gray headed man is Stalin," said Barry.

"You are right," said Kevin.

"Must be something very important to get these two together out here in nowhere."

After the men boarded the automobiles and left, Barry and Kevin walked around the plane, checking everything, went into the front of the cargo compartment, and slept until the late afternoon.

At about three, a large truck came groaning down the road. Inside were what seemed like hundreds of jerry cans of gasoline. Evidently they had hired some locals to help with the fueling. Barry and Kevin each gathered up a chamois and went out onto each wing to supervise the refueling. With the locals manhandling the cans up onto the wing and passing the cans from hand to hand, it took two hours to refuel. They checked the oil, topped up each oil tank and agreed that the plane was ready to go.

In a cloud of dust and clashing gears the great truck reared and surged getting started up the road. It soon disappeared over the rise, but the dust cloud it raised took almost fifteen minutes to dissipate.

With the last light of dusk, they opened a food box the cook had sent along and enjoyed a sliced chicken sandwich with real American mayonnaise. They took their Atabrine with the canteen water.

"I don't know about you, but I could use some more sleep," said Kevin.

"Me too," said Barry, as they walked up the slanting metal floor toward their mats and sleeping bags. Whether they were sleepy or just tired, they quickly dropped off. No bird sounds, no insect noises, no wind noise. No noise at all, except for the occasional tink of a metal part cooling after the sunset.

"Wake up, Kevin, did you hear that?" whispered Barry.

"Yeah," said Kevin as he rolled over and took up his .45.

Silently, they crept to the aircraft door. In the moonlight, they could see two figures under the left wing.

Before either of them could say another word, one of the men used a screwdriver to begin removing a panel on the bottom of the wing.

"What should we do?" asked Barry.

"We are here all alone, there may be more of them backing these two up," said Kevin.

"Do you suppose they are trying to disable the plane or something like fixing it so we cannot make it all the way back. That would make a fine mess over the hump."

"We'd better do something. If we don't jump them soon, they may do something that we can't fix."

"Let's take the chance that they have more standing by. Do you have your flashlight?"

"Sure."

"OK, let's jump down, rather than use the ladder. I will swing the door and you go first. If they try to shoot it out, try not to hit the plane. Let's go on the count of three."

As Kevin swung the door open, Barry jumped the eight feet to the ground. Kevin was just a second or two behind. They both landed on their feet, but both fell forward to their knees. Their flashlights immediately illuminated the two men, who seemed shocked to see them there. Both of them dropped their tools and held up their hands, looking like they expected to be shot on the spot.

Kevin ordered the men to go forward and lie down on the ground. He quickly determined that they were not armed, but he kept them on the ground.

Kevin, it looks like they were trying to mess with the transfer valve inboard of the outboard tank. They obviously know what they are doing. What do they look like, here, let me get a look. These guys could be Mongols or Russians.

"Tovarich? Tovarich? Ruskyi?"

"Da. Da," said the one on the left.

"Kevin, we have big trouble here. If the Russians sent these two to sabotage the plane, the PM is in grave danger. We need to warn him and get the hell out of here. We are in no way equipped to shoot it out with a squad of Russians, let alone whatever number they have here."

"Well, we can't even leave the plane to go warn our men. If we fire warning shots, it may bring the whole Russian contingent down on us and them. I'll go get our people. You guard these guys. If I'm not back in forty five minutes, prepare to get the hell out of here."

"OK, but be careful, no telling how many of them are on that road or watching it."

"OK."

Kevin left at a rapid walk, not using the flashlight in his left hand and keeping a firm grip on his .45 in the other.

There was a little hill between the airstrip and the compound where the meeting was taking place. As Kevin topped the hill, he could see the whole area. Two hundred yards down the dirt road was the main building. Two guards stood outside the door on the side he could see. As he got within a hundred yards, one of the guards called out, "Halt, who goes there?"

"Captain Gallagher, I am alone."

"Come forward and be recognized. Keep your hands up."

Kevin holstered his .45 and raised his hands and walked toward the compound. The only light was what was available inside and came through the windows. When he got fifty yards closer, the guard's flashlight came on.

When he was about ten feet away, the guard asked, "What is the problem, Captain."

"I need to see the big guy. We caught two men trying to sabotage the plane."

The other guard, obviously not one of his party, gasped. He obviously understood English, even though he must be Russian, thought Kevin.

The Russian turned and knocked on the door. A guard on the inside opened it. The other man spoke in Russian to him. He expressed shock and fear. The English guard said to Kevin, "Come in, I'll take you upstairs."

The guard tapped softly on the right double door. A voice inside spoke in Russian. The guard opened the door and let Kevin in.

"Captain Gallagher, what is the matter," asked the PM.

"Sir, Barry and I caught two men messing with the plane. We think they were trying to sabotage the fuel delivery system. Barry is holding them at gun point."

"Great Caesar!" said the PM.

A man at the table leaned over and spoke something softly in Russian to the man opposite the PM. Kevin recognized him instantly. "Holy Smoke, it really is Stalin himself."

Stalin spoke something to his interpreter. The man said to the PM, "Sir, I have advised His Excellency what has been said. He feels we should go immediately to see to this matter. The automobiles will be brought around."

Too quickly to decide otherwise, the whole party began to leave the room. Everyone seemed quite frightened. Even Stalin was not his usually stony self.

The Russians got into two cars and the English party and Kevin piled into the others. The trip to the airstrip took all of forty seconds. The four cars raised clouds of dust on the road and as they swung into a line parallel to the airplane. Everyone jumped out. Clear demarcation lines between the Russians and the English party appeared. The PM and Stalin with his interpreter approached Barry.

"Tell me what you have, Captain," the PM said to Barry.

"Kevin and I jumped these two guys after they started to take the access panel under the fuel valve off, sir."

With all the flashlights and the car lights, the area was well lit up, but the dust of the hurried arrivals of the cars had not yet cleared.

"Whose men are these, Your Excellency?" the PM asked Stalin.

His interpreter spoke to the Russian quietly. Stalin spoke to one of his men in Russian. Then the Russian officer approached the two men. He looked at them carefully and spoke. They replied in Russian.

"They say they are Khazakstani railroad mechanics who were paid to do this by a man who spoke to them in a public tavern in town. They did not get a look at his face."

The officer spoke again to the men. Each reached slowly into a pocket and withdrew a large wad of Russian rubles.

With that, Stalin walked toward the men. As he got within six feet or so, he drew a pistol from his tunic and shot each man a point blank range. Everyone gasped. No one knew exactly what to do, or even approximately what to do. To draw a weapon in the presence of the PM was a grave matter. Stalin stood with the smoking pistol held in front of him for a moment, and then put it back in his tunic. He spoke sharply to his interpreter.

"Your Excellency, Master Stalin begs your pardon and apologizes for this episode. The men have been punished. He asks your forgiveness for his abruptness. He suggests that we reinforce the armed guard around the plane and return to the compound to continue the meeting."

"Tell his Excellency that we need to confer a moment. Ask him to board his automobile and pull away down the road a bit. We will respond shortly."

The interpreter repeated the PM's message to Stalin. He thought for a moment and then spoke to his interpreter. The man said, "We will do so. His Excellency is greatly embarrassed by this provocation. Again he begs your pardon and apologizes."

"Yes, yes," said the PM.

The Russians got back into their automobiles and pulled down the road about a hundred yards.

The Group Captain said: "I don't like it, sir. If we stay, there is no telling what they might do. They have us greatly outnumbered even though we are in neutral territory. They couldn't muster many, but we have only a few. I say we depart immediately."

The PM wrinkled his brow, chomped on his unlit cigar and turned his questioning eyes on Kevin.

"Could you make an immediate night take off, Captain Gallagher?"

"Yes, sir, we are fully refueled and ready."

"This is very tense, sir," said his senior aide. He had strong military bearing even though he wore civilian clothes.

"If anything should happen to you here under these circumstances, it might change the course of the whole war, not to mention the next hundred years of history. I don't like to retreat, but your safety is my primary concern, sir. This could be that Stalin shot those men to shut them up. He may have planned this whole thing. I say, let me walk down to the Russian autos, tell them that you are indisposed by the stress of this event and would rather continue the discussion later. He may be completely free of responsibility, but our reports confirm that he has used the most diabolical means to achieve and hold onto power. The extent of the purges already reported to us..."

"Yes, yes, I know," said the PM.

"Sir, he could have planes chase us down if this really is an assassination attempt," said one of the other aides.

"Not much chance of finding us over this desert at night. The Russians do not have some of the things we have, you know. I think if we could get out, we could be back to the peak of the hump by six in the morning."

"Alright, dammit, let's go," said the PM. Send the autos back. Carl, you go and tell Stalin exactly what you proposed earlier. "Captain Gallagher, get us out of here."

Kevin looked aside at the bodies of the two men, face down in the night.

"I guess we'll never know for sure," he thought.

He and Barry split up the walk around, each man seeing that his side of the plane was airworthy.

In about two minutes, Group Captain Hollister returned, got out of his car, spoke a word to the driver and watched to see that the auto went toward the Russians before he turned and sprinted to the waiting C-46. As he reached the ladder, Kevin started to crank the port engine. The starboard, number two, was already idling. The first cylinder caught and chuffed out a great belch of blue smoke. Kevin brought up the RPMs to one thousand as soon as he saw oil pressure on the gauge. They taxied quickly to the runway while Barry checked the magnetos on the roll. Without hesitating at the end of the runway, Kevin pushed the throttles up to full takeoff power. Down the sandy runway they pounded. Swirls of sandy clouds followed them. Not even a light could be seen in the direction of the Russians. At eighty knots, Barry pulled back on the yoke. About four seconds later, the big plane left the ground.

"Positive rate of climb, gear coming up."

"Back to climb power, whew, that was tense. Let's go home, Kevin."

Kevin looked over at his partner.

"I wouldn't have believed this if you told me," he said.

"Sure, you would. Would I lie to you?" Barry joked.

"No," said Kevin. They smiled at each other.

"Which way was that first mountain?" asked Barry.

"No chance we'll see it in this darkness. I can't see a light on the ground anywhere."

"We have ten hours of this, remember. The mountain was two forty from the field and about eight miles. Let's hold this heading until we get to ten thousand and then set course for Chabua."

After they had put everyone on oxygen, and climbed the rest of the way up to eighteen thousand, they cruised quietly for about an hour.

The first realization that he was standing at his right was when Kevin saw the unlit cigar in a hand. The PM put his hands on the shoulders of the two pilots.

"I wish to express my personal gratitude to you both. That took sang froid. I am sure the rest of the group wants me to extend their thanks, too. By the way, you must never mention this to anyone, unless on strictest orders, you understand."

"Yes, sir," they said together.

He gave each of them a pat on the shoulder, withdrew his hands, placed his cigar in his mouth with great relish, and said quietly.

"Let's go home, fellows."

.

3

MR. PEANUT

The events in Chapter 3 really happened, but the characters are creations.

******

It was after three in the afternoon when Kevin and Barry were summoned to the Colonel's office. His office was a square on the hard packed crushed limestone of the apron, with a beat up square of khaki canvas for a sun shield. The China summer was ninety degrees. Occasionally the fumes of 115/145 octane aviation fuel stifled breath until it dissipated.

"Captains Goldwater and Gallagher reporting as ordered, sir," Barry said.

"At ease," said Colonel Kaigler. "Are you rested from your trip over?"

"Yes, sir," Kevin said. "We even got some 'egguz' at the shack this morning. Those Chinese are mighty enterprising to adapt to our culture so quickly. Who would imagine ham and fried eggs here in China?"

"Just so," said the Colonel. "These people, with their thousands of years of traditions are amazingly fast at adapting to change. Have you had your 'met' briefing?"

"We have," said Barry.

"Most trips are touchy enough with the turbulence and ice on the westbound trip over the hump, but this time, you have something additional to worry about. You will be taking American wounded for treatment at the General Hospital at Jorhat. These men have dysentery so bad they will die of dehydration if they do not get sulfa soon and more intravenous salts. We airlifted them out of Burma yesterday. Two more died last night. Go as soon as your ship is fueled. Don't turn back for anything. One of your passengers is General Stillwell, himself. You will have a Doctor from Jorhat and two nurses aboard. Once you depart, maintain radio silence until you are within fifty miles of Chabua. No fighter escort tonight, I'm afraid. Big doings east of here made all warplanes unavailable for your escort. Have a safe trip and good luck."

They each saluted and turned into the hot China sun.

The B-24 was cooking in the sun. Waves of heat could be seen above the wings as they walked toward Mr. Peanut. The little stick man with the peanut body had been painted on the side of this particular Liberator the night he became their ship. One of the fellows had a can of peanuts in the squad bay where they were playing gin. When Barry and Kevin arrived with the new plane, everyone piled out to the flight line to meet their new companion at arms. One of the fellows had brought the can with him in the jeep as they went out to greet Kevin and Barry and inspect the new Lib. As the can of peanuts was passed around, it seemed appropriate to name the new plane after Mr. Peanut. Now with eleven hundred hours on the tachs and fifty one missions over the hump, it was a veteran.

Because the fueling took so long with hand pumps and chamois for filters, the fueling had started before dawn. Now the fuel was expanding in the tanks and dripping from the vents onto the crushed stones of the apron.

Their manifest of passengers had been loaded before they reached the airplane. Nurses in khaki went from litter to litter, making last minute arrangements. There were sixty one wounded. The fuselage looked like a crowded hospital ward aboard ship as they walked its length to reach the cockpit.

They busied themselves with pre-flight checks and checklists, gear securely stowed and strapped down. Everything had to be secured before takeoff. With no flight engineer, they would have their hands full from engine start to landing.

Kevin took out his binoculars and focused on the tower. Waves of mirage heat wafted over the runway. A soldier walked out onto the deck at the level of the third floor of the tower, and raised a green flag.

"Engine start," called Barry. "Prime number one."

He looked out the side window to assure that a lineman was standing by with an extinguisher. Satisfied that his man was there at the ready, he watched the fuel pressure build up on the gauge. When it hit twenty pounds per square inch, he called "Clear, number one is hot," and switched on the magnetos. His finger flicked up on the starter switch.

The starter deep within the cowling of the number one engine whined a few seconds and then its big four blade prop began to turn, slowly at first, then after ten blades, with a belch of blue smoke, it coughed and settled into a rough idle.

Once the oil pressure was up into the green, Barry called for engine number two. When the four engines were contentedly rumbling, he turned to Kevin and said, "Let's go home."

At his signal, the linemen fell back. The great plane was about to taxi. At the signal from the tower, they pushed the four throttles forward a bit and the wheels broke from their rest and began to roll. From the apron to the runway threshold was about four thousand feet. Barry and Kevin used the time efficiently and were ready to go when they got to the runway threshold.

At the tower, a green flag was run up the flag pole. Barry gave a questioning glance at Kevin. Kevin responded with a thumbs up.

Brakes set. Mixtures full forward. Propellers to high pitch. Superchargers to high. All gauges normal. Now it was time to go. Barry eased the four throttles forward. Revolutions came up steadily. Sometime before the throttles were against the forward stops and the props were screaming their strongest, he released the brakes and the big plane began its lumbering takeoff run. Four thousand feet down the runway, the call of Vr came. All gauges still normal. Now Kevin applied back pressure to the yoke on his side. In a couple of seconds, the nose wheel lifted off of the crushed stone runway. About eight seconds later, in front of a cloud of limestone dust, the main gear lifted and flight began.

With the wheels diverging under the wings to their stowed positions, they began a slow shallow turn to the left and departed Kunming once again. The afternoon sun was at their backs and the view was magnificent. The big plane eased up to ten thousand feet, where they reduced the rate of climb to one hundred fifty feet per minute for a cruise climb to their cruising altitude of eighteen thousand feet. Several extra cylinders were necessary to provide enough oxygen for all on board. The temperature fell steadily as they climbed. Soon, it was chilly, even in the hot China summer.

"They really sprang this on us, didn't they?" asked Kevin.

"Yeah, I wish they had told us that we would be bringing back General Stillwell and the others. Not that it would have changed anything. Maybe it's better that we didn't know. I would have been scared out of my wits."

"Did you see him as we walked through," asked Kevin.

"Yes, he looked like a ghost," said Barry.

"Those guys got out of Burma by the skins of their teeth. They really look eaten up."

"Clark told me that Colonel Harris chose us because he considered us the best navigators of all the pilots in his command," said Barry.

"No kidding," said Kevin. "I had no idea."

"This flight will end after dark and I guess he thought, without fighter escort, and with radio silence, navigation was a strong factor."

"Remind me to thank him for his confidence in us," said Kevin.

The under cast began as wisps, then patches, then areas, then the holes closed and it was solid below. Even though they could not see through, Kevin and Barry knew that the sharp peaks below reached up closer each minute. Once they were three hours out, the slopes would be receding and then to Chabua.

It was dark now above. Stars were clear in the night sky. They knew from a star fix that they were about half way home. Then, over a period of minutes, the under cast rose to touch the belly of Mr. Peanut, creep up its sides and swallow the plane. Now they were on instruments. Smooth whiteness whisked past the windscreen as they plowed ahead.

"Is everything alright with the passengers?" asked Barry.

"No complaints," said Kevin.

"Why don't you take it for a few minutes while I go back and visit," said Barry.

"I have it. Take your time," said Kevin.

The cargo area was full of cots, built up with aluminum uprights into triple deck bunks. The men in the bunks were all emaciated. Their eyes were sunken, but in each man's eyes gleamed the pleasure of a job well done and hope for tomorrow, and maybe someday an end to this terrible war.

"Dr. Hash, how are things?"

"Fine, no urgent problems," he said. "How much longer? I have one man who needs an amputation below the knee. He has gangrene and has a high fever. He will have to go directly to surgery."

"Is he conscious?" asked Barry.

"Yes, but we have him doped up a bit because of the pain."

"Would it help if I spoke to him?" asked Barry.

"Sure wouldn't hurt, Captain. The guys appreciate your coming up to get them."

Sergeant Wales was drowsy with medication. He was dark haired, heavy bearded, and now weighed about one hundred twenty pounds instead of his usual one sixty. He gave the impression of a man determined, and now even as sick as he was, you got the feeling that he was a friend you could count on.

"Thank God we have such people," thought Barry to himself, "Guide us safely to our destination."

"Hello, sergeant, doing OK?"

"Yes, sir. Thanks for the ride."

"Don't mention it. Uncle is paying for the gas, we just aim this thing."

"No kidding, Captain, is flying that easy?"

"This plane has a heart, Sergeant Wales. I sometimes feel that it knows the way home. You get some rest now. We'll have you to Chabua in the middle of the night."

He smiled and his eyes began to slowly close.

Barry gave him a pat on the shoulder.

As they went back forward, he asked Dr. Hash, "What happened to his leg?"

"Started out as a blister on his foot. They were all forced to march. No time to stop. Japs were dogging them all the way, but never caught up. He carried the rear of a litter with a wounded buddy over three hundred miles. When they got to an area where they could be evacuated, his foot was gangrenous. They tied it off, but it has spread now up his leg, so we will have to take it off just below the knee. He should have a normal life, once he gets used to having a wooden leg."

"What did he do before the war? What will he go back to?"

"He was a postal letter carrier. No more of that, for sure, but he will probably go with his father's small construction company and help build houses in Staunton."

They both looked back at the bay of ailing men. The drone of the engines continued its ever present embrace around them.

"Pretty decent of you to volunteer to come over and fly back with these men, Dr. Hash. How many trips over the hump for you now?"

"Forty one," he said.

"It's in honor to fly with you, sir," said Barry. They shook hands.

Barry turned back toward the cockpit. Just as he did, the number three engine backfired. Barry saw the flash through the small observation port as he passed.

By the time he got back into his seat, the number three was barking regular flashes out the exhaust stack.

"Cylinder head temp is falling on number three. Carb heat isn't helping. RPMs falling to fifteen hundred," said Kevin as Barry settled into his seat.

"Better cage it," said Barry.

With an upward reach, Kevin hit the feather switch for number three and with his left hand pulled back the number three throttle and mixture to the stops. The propeller to the right of the cockpit spun down to a stop, its blades aligned with the direction of travel. Now on three engines, the B-24 maintained altitude with a little up trim and maintained heading with a little rudder trim, but the airspeed dropped from two twenty five to one eighty.

"Better refigure our time to Chabua and estimate our position," said Barry.

"Will do," said Kevin. "Fuel is OK, plenty enough. I make our time to Chabua as one hour fifteen minutes. That puts us about fifty miles east of Razor Ridge. Should be OK if there is no further trouble. I'll go reassure the passengers."

"OK," said Barry. "I've got it."

Just as Kevin swung out of his seat, the number two engine backfired with a flash. Still in the clouds, the flash was extra bright in the night. No one with his eyes open could have missed it.

"All engines have carburetor heat on," said Kevin. "I turned it on when the first indication of icing occurred. Let's have a look at the wings."

As he swung the flashlight along the right wing, they both saw about a half inch of rime ice and even in the clouds, they could see the precipitation, some frozen into ice crystals, some still looking wet.

"Airspeed is dropping some. If we don't get out of this ice soon, we will have to start down to maintain safe speed."

"What do I tell the Doctor?" asked Kevin.

"Tell him to dump all unnecessary weight, starting with used up oxygen cylinders. Tell him if the problem doesn't get worse, we will make it OK."

The airspeed had now dropped to one twenty. Came a time when, to maintain one twenty Barry had to begin a gradual descent, now two hundred feet per minute.

Twenty minutes later, without much dialogue between the pilots, the number four engine began backfiring, and predictably about five minutes later, they had to cage it and feather its prop like the number three and number two. Now they were descending through seventeen thousand feet at one hundred twenty miles per hour at a rate of five hundred feet per minute, still in the clouds.

"No more ice buildup," said Kevin.

"That's good, we can't take much more bad news," said Barry.

"Do you reckon we will clear Razor Ridge?"

"Depending on exactly where we cross it, we need at least fourteen thousand feet. If we go below that, it depends on where we cross it as to whether we will have enough altitude."

"Sure hope we break out before we get down to that altitude," said Kevin. Barry looked over and nodded.

Dr. Hash called on the interphone. "We have jettisoned everything loose back here, I don't know of a thing more we can throw out. What is the situation, Captain?"

Barry and Kevin shared a glance. There was a pause. Barry keyed his mike, "Doctor Hash, I won't minimize the situation. We are on one engine, maintaining safe airspeed, descending at five hundred feet per minute. If we clear Razor Ridge ahead, we have a good chance of reaching Chabua. We make it about five more minutes to Razor Ridge. It might be a good time to pray a little."

"Roger, Captain, thanks, I know you and Kevin are doing your best."

"Call when you need to, Dr. Hash," said Barry.

"Will do," said Dr. Hash.

The plane was much quieter, with only the outboard left engine. The snow swished about the skin of Mr. Peanut. The altimeters in front of Barry and Kevin agreed on sixteen thousand feet. Long tense minutes passed. Then they began to break clear of the clouds at about fourteen six. To the right was a peak above their altitude. Ahead was another rising in the windscreen. They steered to the left and squirted through a valley in the ridge, just three or four hundred feet above the rocks.

"Whew!" said Barry.

"Likewise," Kevin replied.

"How far you make Chabua?" asked Barry.

"Should be about a hundred miles," said Kevin after some thought.

"At this rate, if we cannot reduce the descent rate, we won't make it. Better brief the Doctor. Tell him we don't think we will make it. Tell him when we signal, to get as many men forward as can. Jam them together, standing if possible at the front bulkhead. Tell him we will give him about three minutes warning."

"Will do," said Kevin, and started back.

The flashlight showed a little more ice, but not much. That outboard engine was still running at almost top output.

"Please keep it together," he prayed about the number one.

Descent rate was still five hundred feet per minute. Altitude was now ten thousand eight. Twenty minutes to Chabua. Twenty minutes at this descent rate before ground contact, no matter where.

Chabua non-directional beacon had been pulling the ADF needle toward it for an hour. It still stood straight up.

Barry couldn't think of anything additional to do to help retard the descent. He had closed the cowl flaps on numbers three, two and four. The props were feathered. All was as clean as he could make it.

Now out of the blackness came the beacon at Chabua, dead ahead. No other light showed. He knew that their radar would show his approach. They would turn off the beacon as soon as he landed, if he landed.....

Kevin slid into the right seat, "Dr. Hash and the men did a good job of emptying things. I couldn't find a thing to dump."

"I don't think we should get the men up," said Kevin.

"We have a fifty-fifty chance now of making the field. You will have to crank the gear down, Kevin. The hydraulic pumps are both out with the number two and three."

"Just say when," said Kevin.

"Get in position, I will call you," said Barry.

"OK," said Kevin and started for the crank.

In a minute, Barry called: "Start now, let me know when they are all down and locked. I won't use flaps until we are sure we have the field."

"Roger," said Kevin, as he started cranking.

As the wheels came out, the plane slowed more. Some shudders passed through the airframe as it nudged stall speed.

"Gear down and locked," called Kevin.

"Get up here," said Barry.

As Kevin swung into his seat, he could see that they were on about a six mile final for runway two zero.

"Will we make it?" he asked Barry.

"It will be close," said Barry. "No flaps until over the threshold. We have to hold a hundred on final. Stay with us."

Their eyes shot to the airspeed indicators. Right on one hundred. Nothing to do but watch. No change in control surfaces would help. The nose up trim was right.

"What if we land short?" asked Kevin.

"Old fuel drum dump north of the threshold. All empty, but not a good place to land."

There was nothing left to do but hold all the controls where they were and wait.

Some say your life flashes before your eyes at such moments. Not here. These two men watched every foot of the way. There might need to be some last second adjustment or movement of the controls to get that last few feet of flight.

Short final. Barry flicked on the landing lights. The number 20 shown at the end of the runway. It looked high in the windscreen.

Just as they were certain that they would sink into the drum storage area, Barry reached over and pulled the flap lever. Mr. Peanut heaved up. Barry answered with a push forward on the yoke. The airspeed dropped, and they seemed to hover as they made those last few feet to the threshold. The plane settled with a thump on all three wheels. Barry quickly pulled the throttle back on the still hard working number one to keep them from yawing off of the runway. They coasted quietly in the dark. As they slowed they could see the equipment lining the runway. It looked like the whole complement of the base was on hand, at the ready.

As they slowed to a stop, Barry pulled the mixture of number one. A muted cheer could be heard in the rear. It took a while before they could get out of their seats. Mr. Peanut had done his job again.

4

DETROIT METRO

Ted always wondered at how different the airport and the flight deck looked in the dark. What was an expanse of black and white pavement, yellow lines and white lines, became a black velvet canvas with red, yellow, green, white and blue lights, each with its own message, some steady, some blinking, some rotating, some flashing. The flight deck of the 747-400 was a cave of black. As he stepped through the flight deck door, he stopped and took a minute for his eyes to adjust to the absence of light. Then he took a step forward and touched the cabin light switch. The area lights came up and he stepped over to the locker and hung up his cap and uniform jacket.

Detroit Metro was dark and clear, but all he could see from the cockpit window was the nearby wall of the terminal and the jetway leading to the forward entry door to his left. He reached over and flipped the master switch to "on." Immediately a hundred colored eyes beamed at him, each a pinpoint of light in the dark, each with a message for him. These over ocean flights required a longer preflight than the city to city flights, so he began to read and check off items based on the fuel manifest and galley manifest. Two hundred sixty thousand pounds of Jet-A. Enough to fuel the generators for a city of seventy thousand people for a month. Twelve hundred meals, breakfasts, lunches, dinners. Snacks and beverages for the flight. Face towels to steam for that last minute refresher before landing tomorrow morning at Kaitek.

A night departure is special. How many instructors and pilots in his career had made the same observation? Sure, it's special. Everything is reversed, kind of like a negative of a photograph, but it's more than that.

The high altitude charts for the route over Juneau were in the rack by his side, properly folded. The coordinates for the checkpoints on the route were carefully input into the navigation radio and the GPS. Since GPS, there was no excuse for not knowing where you were. Satellite navigation, Buck Rogers stuff when he was growing up, now real, and right on the money all the time. No need for the radio receivers to strain to pick up the signal of a distant non-directional beacon far across the waters. He remembered the nights when he had flown the Atlantic earlier, and they all strained to hear the Irish jigs broadcast from Radio Shannon. Now the GPS receivers got their stuff directly from orbiting satellites. You were never out of "sight" of three or four and the signal was reliable as rain.

Since this was his leg, even the captain's arrival on the flight deck didn't break his concentration. Preparation for his flight was the focus. Four hundred souls, all that baggage, all that fuel, all that airframe, all those parts, all straining to get them there.

"Detroit Metro clearance delivery, Northwest 452, Gate 22, Kaitek, information Zulu, ready to pushback in twelve minutes."

"Roger Northwest 452, wind 285 at 12, altimeter 30.02, visibility greater than 6, ceiling unlimited, temperature 15, dew point 10, expect Runway 2 center, departure on 118.2, squawk 4011, contact ground control on 125.6 when ready to taxi."

"Roger, Detroit Metro Clearance", he said and repeated the clearance.

Engine start sure was different in a 747 from the days of DC-6s he remembered. On such flights, with the radial engines, a ground crew member stood by with a fire extinguisher, now the turbines began their acceleration to a whining blindness with the smoothness of polished metal. Soon the steady whine permeated every part of the ship as the tug pushed them away from Gate 22.

Following the imbedded yellow taxi lights was easy, but once out of the protective lighting of the gate area, the challenge of progressive taxiing to your runway threshold at a large complicated airport like Detroit Metro was daunting. He never felt relaxed about taxiing here.

Finally, at the runway threshold, all the preparation focused. "Northwest 452, clear for takeoff, Runway 2 center, have a good flight."

"Roger, Tower, thanks, 452 is rolling."

Having all that thrust come up was still a rush. In the time between takeoff clearance and when the airspeed came alive, there was time for the flight engineer to check all the thrust gages, fuel flow meters, pressure gages, but all that was monitored by computers to back him up. No warnings flashed, all was well. The heartbeat of the great aircraft grew as it accelerated down the runway.

He never got over it. No matter how many thousands of hours in his logbook. A maximum gross weight takeoff at night was still a magnificent performance. Just think of all the designers who conceived and designed this airplane, all the metal workers who cut and stamped its skin and spars, all the assemblers who put every rivet in place, bucked properly, the inspectors, upholsterers, painters, the avionics techs who installed and tested the radios and other electrical wiring, the engine builders who carefully put the engines together, one blade at a time, all the people who tried, pushed, pulled, carried, brushed, filled, polished, and lifted to get this airplane where it was. Those who loaded the baggage, the fuel, the food, those who checked the fluids carried in the hydraulic system and the onboard water supply. Even his own walk around inspection before he boarded was part of the preparation for this flight. And now, in this accelerating rush, it all came together. Here and now, this magnificent airplane was giving us everything it had. Full throttle. Slight backpressure on the yoke. Airspeed approaching 140, the direction changes some from forward only to forward and up. The runway as if by magic began to fall away, the perspective darkened as the night sky filled the windshield.

"Here we come, Keeper of the stars, we are again visiting your domain."

Full power. Confirm vertical speed. OK. Gear coming up. All that rubber, steel, hydraulic fluid, swinging up into the wings and fuselage, cleaning up the underbelly for climb.

"Go, baby, go," he thought, almost leaning forward in his seat to urge it on. Flaps to 5. Set climb power, he thought as he pulled back slightly on the thrust levers. Coming through one thousand feet.

"Detroit Metro Departure, Northwest 452 with you climbing through one thousand, squawking 4011."

"Roger Northwest 452, climb on runway heading to one zero thousand, ten thousand."

"Runway heading to one zero, ten thousand, Northwest 452."

The lights of even so magnificent a city as Detroit must fade into distance, and so they did. Ahead lay the vast plains and Canada. The vertical speed indicator settled back to 1000 feet per minute. Eight hundred fifty five thousand pounds, lifted by the thrust of four engines and that great wing sticking out into the night.

"Go, baby, go."

"Northwest 452, turn left to three one zero degrees, climb to Flight Level two four zero and contact Chicago Center on 133.45, good night."

"Left to three one zero, out of four thousand for Flight level two four zero, and center on 133.45. Thanks departure, Northwest 452."

"Go, baby go!"

HAVE AN ICE DAY

"Akron-Canton Approach, Cessna November one zero zero mike mike, IFR to Lunken."

"Cessna One zero zero mike mike, I show you squawking 2357 at eighteen hundred, confirm."

"Squawking 2357, Cessna one hundred mike mike is climbing through nineteen hundred."

"Roger, one hundred mike mike, turn left to heading of 210 and climb and maintain six thousand feet, report reaching."

"One hundred mike mike left to two one zero and climbing to six thousand."

We were on our way on a dark gray day. The outside temperature was five Celsius on the ground and as we climbed through four thousand, the thermometer read zero degrees C.

Nick Southall, my instructor, was a British national, over to the U.S. for a while to acquire his Certified Flight Instructor, Instrument rating and build a little time. My friend Mike Mealey had gotten the two of us together when he heard that I was making this round robin trip to Akron, Ohio, Cincinnati, Ohio and return. It was early in February and winter was in full swing in northern Ohio.

As we passed through five thousand, we began to pick up ice on the leading edges.

I said to Nick, "Beginning to ice up."

He acknowledged with a nod.

By the time we got to six thousand and leveled, there was about an eighth of an inch on the leading edges and the windshield was beginning to frost over in the corners. Since the ice was continuing to build, I asked Nick over the intercom if we shouldn't report the ice and ask for a different altitude. He nodded.

"Akron-Canton Approach, one hundred mike mike is level now at six thousand, picking up ice. Any chance for a different altitude?"

"One hundred mike mike, we show you twenty south of Akron-Canton, we cannot give you a different altitude just now due to traffic. Stand by."

"Roger, Akron-Canton, one hundred mike mike standing by."

Eight or so minutes later, the ice was at least one quarter of an inch and still building.

"Akron-Canton approach, one hundred mike mike is still picking up ice. Any chance for lower?"

"Negative, one hundred mike mike, traffic below you. Contact Columbus Approach now on one two six point six."

"Roger, one hundred mike mike over to Columbus approach on one two six point six. Good day."

On the new frequency, I called: "Columbus approach, Cessna November one hundred mike mike with you level at six thousand."

"Roger, November one hundred mike mike, maintain six thousand."

"Columbus approach, one hundred mike mike has picked up about a half inch of ice on the leading edges, we need lower."

"Roger, one hundred mike mike, cannot give you lower at this time due to traffic, stand by."

For another fifteen minutes, the ice continued to build. Now we were at three quarters of an inch. I had gone to twenty four inches of manifold pressure and twenty four hundred RPMs to hold altitude. Things were getting a bit tense.

"Nick, I have no experience in ice with this aircraft. Do you?"

He shook his head in the negative. "Do you think we should declare an emergency?"

He said, "Not yet, the aircraft seems to be handling it OK. Let's wait a little longer."

By the time another ten minutes had passed, we had an inch on the leading edges. I was getting tenser. The power now was against the stop and I had set the RPMs at twenty five hundred just to hold altitude at one hundred knots. Not a good situation.

"November one hundred mike mike, contact Cincinnati Approach now on one one eight point niner. Good day."

"Roger, Columbus approach, one hundred mike mike over to Cincinnati on one one eight point niner. Good day."

"Cincinnati Approach, Cessna November one hundred mike mike with you level at six thousand, with a load of ice, needing lower."

"Roger, November one hundred mike mike, we show you twenty north of Cincinnati Lunken field, contact Lunken tower now on one one niner point two for vectors. Good day."

"Roger, one hundred mike mike over to Lunken tower on one one niner point two. Good day."

"Lunken Tower, Cessna one hundred mike mike, with a load of ice, needing lower."

"November one hundred mike mike, Lunken Tower, cleared for the ILS Runway two zero Approach at Lunken, circle to land Runway 24, maintain two thousand until established. You may begin your descent now."

"Roger, Lunken Tower, one hundred mike mike is out of six for two thousand at this time. Understand cleared for the ILS Runway two zero Approach, circle to land Runway two four at Lunken."

"One hundred mike mike, say conditions."

"One hundred mike mike has more than an inch of ice on the leading edges, windshield iced over, almost full power, descending at ninety knots."

"Roger, one hundred mike mike, cleared to land, report the marker."

We had gotten out the approach plate for the Runway two zero approach and set all the radios for the proper frequencies. The number one navigation radio was picking up the localizer at Lunken, but we were still below the glide slope. Just as I was about to comment on that, the needle began to descend toward center.

"There's the glide slope," I said.

Nick nodded his agreement.

Down we went at about five hundred feet a minute, still at almost full power.

Just as we broke into visual conditions with about five miles of visibility, I said to Nick, "We need to turn to Runway 24. I can't see through the windshield, so you turn us to the runway and I will make the landing."

He nodded OK.

Nick turned us to line up with runway two four as we sailed down through the restricted visibility. Just about two hundred yards out, he pulled the throttle out. The wing stalled immediately. I jammed the throttle back in. The motor caught and began to rev. It arrested our plummet just at the runway. We touched down without a bounce and rolled quickly toward the tower.

"Wow, one hundred mike mike, that was some landing," said Approach.

"You should have seen it from here," I replied.

We taxied up beyond the tower to the tie down area. We could not see well from the windshield, but we managed to find a spot. As I walked carefully on the snow covered tarmac into the fixed base operator's pilot's lounge, I looked back to see Nick breaking great hunks of ice about an inch and a half thick from the wings. I made myself a promise to never let that much ice build up on a plane again.

6

SYDNEY

"Good evening, ladies and gentlemen. This is Captain Gallagher welcoming you to Northwest Airlines Flight 475 to Hong Kong. Our four hundred series Boeing 747 will make the flight from Sydney to Hong Kong in five hours and ten minutes. I would like to note that among the regular passengers this evening, there is a large group of men who have just attended the World Convocation of the Promise Keepers. Approximately two hundred of the passengers on board are members of this group, and I am too."

So, sit back, enjoy your flight. Hostesses and flight attendants will be serving a meal once we get to cruising altitude. Let us know if you need anything and thank you for flying with Northwest Airlines tonight."

"Sydney Clearance, Northwest 475, Hong Kong Chek Lap Kok, Gate 10, information India, ready for pushback."

"Roger Northwest 475, cleared as filed, expect runway five and expect twenty five thousand ten minutes after departure, departure on 118.75, squawk 4114, altimeter setting thirty decimal zero four, wind is zero five zero at eight, visibility is twenty, ceiling twenty five thousand thin broken, contact ground control on 125.5 when ready to taxi."

"Roger Clearance," said Dave Thomas, the co-pilot, and read back the clearance. Then with a touch on the radio, the frequency of ground control came up.

"Sydney Ground, Northwest 475 at gate 10, ready to taxi."

"Northwest 475, Sydney Ground, good evening. Taxi to Runway 5 by way of taxiway delta, tower on 118.4."

"Roger, Ground, Northwest 475 to Runway five by way of delta."

Now the great airplane really came to life. All engines were running. Lights in the cabin made the big plane a bright sight on the ramp at Sydney. Its great nose wheels turned sharply to align it with the yellow stripe out of the gate area.

In the minutes that followed, the flight deck was criss crossed many times by calls and challenges and answers as the preflight checks were performed.

Then came the magic moment, "Northwest 475, Sydney Tower, cleared for takeoff, fly runway heading."

"Roger, Tower, Northwest 475 is rolling."

At last, with the last glow of twilight, Flight 475 taxied onto Runway 5 and its landing lights came on.

Now it all came together. Kevin was always thrilled and amazed as the great airplane gathered itself up and generated the awesome power to take off. Enough power to run the cars of a great city for a whole day was unleashed in that minute or so that it took to surge, then sprint down the runway. The focus of the efforts of hundreds of people unseen came together in that moment. Kevin could visualize the mechanics who maintain the great planes, standing in the hangars along the airport, glancing up from their work, perhaps wiping the oil from a tool, in time to see the plane make its run toward the sky.

At one hundred forty knots, he eased the yoke back and in five or six seconds, the motion became upward as well as forward. After positive rate of climb was ascertained, with the movement of a bar to his right, in one smooth flow, all of those wheels pulled inward and upward, tucked into metal openings and disappeared. The bird was preening for flight.

"Here we come, Starkeeper. Hold us in your hand tonight."

"Sydney Approach, Northwest 475 off Runway 5 passing through one thousand five hundred."

"Good evening Northwest 475, Sidney Approach, fly runway heading for now, climb and maintain one zero, ten thousand."

"Up to one zero, ten thousand, Northwest 475." As they rose through the twilight, stars came into clearer view. No air traffic ahead in sight, the clearest of nights. What a sight!

"Northwest 475 turn left to zero one zero, join Pacific Airway 36, climb to flight level 330."

"Up to flight level 330, join Pacific 36, Northwest 475, thank you."

Once up to flight level 330, Kevin turned off the seatbelt sign. The great ship then became a dining room, with meals for three hundred fifty being served. The warm smells of bread, cheese, vegetables, and meat filled the cabin. Fine wines were offered. Dinner music was piped into the earphones, quite a different ambiance from the older propeller airliners with their constant din of vibration from the reciprocating engines. Now the turbines whirled in astounding speed, but since they just rotated and did not reciprocate, or move back and forth, ten times the power was applied with one tenth of the noise and essentially no engine vibration.

Flight 475 sailed on through the night. The warmth of the Pacific was far below, now the outside temperature was fifty five below zero. In the second hour, after the passengers had filled their bellies and the in-flight movie was under way, the Global Positioning Systems indicated a ground speed of four hundred sixty knots, a headwind of forty five knots sixteen degrees off the nose to the left and only one thousand sixty three nautical miles to Chek Lap Kok, the new airport at Hong Kong.

With no lights on the sea below to give a reference, the crew flew the great plane by instruments and autopilot. The plane entered instrument meteorological conditions as it slipped into a cloud. The guidance system didn't care if it was in good visibility or cloud, up was still up and over there was where it was going, just as it was told. After another half hour, it was time for the crew to rotate one of its number for a stroll or break. Just as Kevin was about to ask who needed to go first, a call came in on the intercom.

"Captain," called the stewardess in first class.

"Yes, Penny," said Kevin.

"There seems to be smoke in the first class cabin. I double checked and no one is smoking in the seats or in the lavatories. It smells a little hot, too." Her voice was calm, professional.

"Thanks, Penny, we'll check it out."

"Dave, go back and stroll through first class."

"Yes, sir," and Dave unbuckled and squirmed out of his seat to go aft. Just as he got to the flight deck door, the flight attendant from the rear section called.

"Captain, we have smoke back here. Smells hot, could it be the air conditioning?"

"We're checking on it, Melissa. First class reports smoke and an odor, too."

Dave came back in a few minutes. "I don't think it is the air conditioning. It smells different. I remember what a burned out compressor motor smells like. Just the same, I would like to go below and check things there."

"Go ahead," said Kevin.

Kelly Flynn, the engineer, spoke next, a little higher tone than his usual baritone. "Captain, we are losing number two. I have gone to continuous ignition. Fuel flow is normal, thrust is rapidly decreasing to zero."

"Very well. Dave notify ops that we have an engine out and get me a course to the nearest suitable runway just in case."

"Yes, sir," came Dave's prompt reply.

"I'd better tell the passengers," Kevin said.

Just as he was about to key the mike for the speaker system, Kelly interrupted. "Captain, we are losing one and three now. Same condition as number two, and there goes number four. We are a glider."

"Very well, keep doing what you can to relight while I alert the passengers."

"Ladies and gentlemen, this is Captain Gallagher, I regret to inform you that we have lost power on our engines. You may see some flames from the rear of the engines, but do not be alarmed, that does not, repeat, does not mean that the engine is on fire. That is fuel that has not burned properly in the engine and is being ignited as it exhausts from the rear of the engine. We are now at thirty two thousand feet and are gliding toward the nearest airport. Promise keepers, your prayers now would be welcome. Please be assured that we are doing our best up here. Thank you."

"Dave, what is the nearest airport?"

"It's Port Moresby, but we'll never make it, even with our glide ratio and altitude. Better prepare the cabin for ditching at sea."

"Kelly, any luck?"

"No, Captain. Same same. No power. I suggest you jettison fuel to get our gross weight as low as possible."

"Kelly, you take care of fuel jettison. Can you do that and stay on the problem with the engines?"

"Can do," Captain.

"Our altitude is now twenty five thousand. At this rate, we can glide another hundred miles at best. What landmass is nearby, Dave? You check that while I call."

"Mayday, Mayday, Mayday. This is Northwest 475 approximately two hundred fifty miles southeast of Port Moresby. All four engines out. Descending through twenty two thousand now. Preparing for ditching at sea. Any ship in the area of latitude ten degrees five minutes South and One hundred forty five degrees forty minutes east, please call on either 121.5, or 4450 kilohertz. Mayday, Mayday, Mayday."

He touched the button for all of the cabin intercoms. "Ladies, prepare the cabin for a ditching at sea. Reassure the passengers that the water is warm, that we have plenty of rafts, with radios and rations. We estimate landing in approximately fifteen minutes. Call me if you have problems."

"Kelly, having any luck?"

"No, Captain. Everything is just dead. Still on continuous ignition, fuel flows on boost, no thrust."

"Northwest 475, this is Cathay Pacific 145, we are north of you, on our way to Perth. Can we be of service?"

"Thank you Cathay Pacific 145, please guard the frequency. We will notify you if we need you. You could head for Latitude zero zero eight degrees and longitude one four five degrees which is where we estimate ditching."

"Roger, Northwest 475, we will divert. Estimate reaching those coordinates in approximately forty minutes, Cathay 145."

"Northwest 475, this is USS Eisenhower on 4450. Our position is about four hundred nautical miles north west of your estimated ditching position. We are proceeding flank speed that direction. Will dispatch rescue helicopters as soon as within range. Keep us advised and especially advise your landing coordinates when determined. Meantime, we will monitor the frequency. Call us if you need to. Over."

"Roger, USS Eisenhower, thank you, Northwest 475."

"Altitude now sixteen thousand, Kelly, anything?"

"No, Captain."

"Ladies and Gentlemen, I'm sorry to inform you that we are going to have to ditch at sea. We are dumping fuel to lighten our weight, so we can land at a lighter weight. That means we can touch down at a slower speed. Your cabin attendants are well trained in preparing you for this procedure. Please understand that we are doing everything we can up here. The aircraft carrier Eisenhower is proceeding toward our estimated landing site at full speed. If you need help with prayer, please consult your nearest Promise Keeper. If all Promise Keepers would identify yourself by raising your hand, this will give your neighbors some comfort, I hope. Once we complete our landing, please proceed quickly to your assigned exit. It is better to swim for a while than it is to hesitate at the door of the aircraft. We have plenty of life rafts with lights and equipment. Good swimmers are requested to swim away from the aircraft and keep weaker swimmers with you until the rafts are fully inflated and ready to take you aboard. We pilots refer to God sometimes as the Starkeeper. We feel that he watches over us in the air. We take some inspiration from the old spiritual, 'His eye is on the sparrow, and I know He watches me.' Please remember that we are doing everything we can think of to restore power. May God bless you and we will join you in the rafts in a few minutes. Thank you, and good luck."

"I hate to tell them that!" he said. "Altitude is now eleven thousand, crew. Make sure seatbelts tight. We will exit through the overhead door. Dave, be in charge of getting our raft out and inflated, OK?"

"OK, Captain."

"Gentlemen, it has been a privilege to have flown with you. Survivors go and console the widows and orphans, OK?"

"Captain, I am getting power back on number one, now on number three. Number four is showing signs of life. I can't explain it. Fuel flows coming up toward normal. Try the power quadrant for response."

Kevin moved the power levers up a bit and sure enough, there was a surge of power, enough to level off. "Does it look like we should climb, Kelly?"

"Roger, Captain, you should have full power on one, three and four. Number two is still quiet."

"Give me a heading to Port Moresby, Dave."

"Roger."

"Ladies and Gentlemen, no doubt you have felt the surge of power. We now have three of our engines producing normal thrust. Number two, the inboard left engine is still out. This aircraft will fly just fine on three, so we are proceeding with caution toward Port Moresby. Please keep your life vests on until advised. Thank you."

"Northwest 475, this is Port Moresby Control. Indonesian authorities have reported a large volcano eruption just west of your position, which began approximately two hours ago. You may be in that portion of the cloud that has insufficient oxygen to support combustion. We monitored your latest briefing to the crew. We will have all equipment standing by. Based on your speed and course, we estimate you in Port Moresby in thirty two minutes. Glad to be expecting you. Over."

"Roger, Port Moresby. Northwest 475 is still on the gauges. We are cruising at twenty thousand and estimate your airport in three zero minutes."

"Landing on three is a bit tricky, said Kevin to Dave, but we can handle it. Get the conditions at Port Moresby for me will you?"

"Sure, Captain."

Just then, the great plane flew out of the cloud. Dave took out a flashlight and shined it at the windscreens. They were translucent in the centers, but the margins could still be seen through.

"Just like sandpaper, Captain. Much more and we would have to land blind."

"Good enough," said Kevin.

When they landed at Port Moresby, there was no paint on the leading edges, the impellers in the engines were trashed by the abrasive effects of the airborne lava, and the windows were sandblasted over most of their areas, but the landing gear came down just like always and the big ship settled onto the runway with its usual grace. Most of Port Moresby was there to watch.

7

CHASE CITY

Only the remnant of a bird's egg betrayed the fact that anyone or anything had been inside the hut since the technician had last closed and sealed the door six months ago. On its last semi-annual check, the technician had to replace three tubes in the ancient but reliable Chase City non-directional beacon. After getting the rest of his tools from the van and working for approximately forty-five minutes, checking the various circuits and back-up circuits, he saw Chick Clayton come in the hut's tiny door.

"Hi, Chick."

"Hey, Sammy, how you been?"

"Oh, not too bad. I've checked two of these today and I'm just about ready to go on down to Petersburg to stay over for a swing through the tidewater area."

"How's the old guy doing?"

"Not too bad for a '37 model. So far only two tubes needed to be replaced and they're not really burned out, just weak."

"I guess the State wants them to be reliable enough so we'll replace them before it's absolutely necessary. I think I'll get back to the Bellanca if you don't need me, Sammy."

"No, I'll be through in here in a little while. It was good to see you again, Chick."

"Yeah, me too," said Clayton, as he ducked to go out through the abbreviated door of the small corrugated metal building that housed the transmitter. Outside, almost automatically, Chick looked up and observed the shallow Christmas-tree-like array of the antenna for the non-directional beacon which radiated out from the central pedestal approximately fifty feet in a circular pattern.

Chick remembered when the Civil Aeronautics Authority contacted the previous owner of the Chase City Airport to notify him that the CAA had decided to place a non-directional beacon at Chase City. In those days, non-directional beacons were the most modern navigation aids to aircraft since the range transmitters were being phased out. After that came radar and the VOR system, all over the country.

In these times, thought Chick, people aren't going to be relying on the old Chase City NDB much. Hardly anyone who isn't a local pilot is going to land at Chase City. Not that the thirty nine hundred foot asphalt runway was unfriendly, but, in a small rural farming community in Virginia, one can't expect too many aircraft borne visitors.

With the price of aviation gasoline being what it is and the deep slump in general aviation, it's really surprising that the amount of activity exists that does exist, he thought.

Well, with three active students and one plane for rent, Chase City Airport certainly wasn't a bustling metropolitan airdrome. Chick kind of smiled and shook his head when he remembered through the years how sparse aviation really had been in his little rural corner of Piedmont Virginia. Over the years, having been an early licensee as an airframe and power plant mechanic and a certified flight instructor, with the repair work and repainting from which he gathered a good regional reputation, the occasional instruction, as well as the one or two aircraft he managed to restore and sell each year, Chick had eked out a living, which entirely suited him even though he had accumulated very little.

He was one of those consummate mechanics who has always got a wrench turning or some tool at work, whether it is in his mind or in his hand, and he only ceased to think about the string of projects currently under way when the lights went out and sleep finally came. As Chick went back through the opening he had left in the large hangar doors and into the hangar, he could smell the fresh paint on the Bellanca he had finished only a few hours before.

"Nice result," he thought. "That polyurethane paint is the berries. Nothing like the dope and silver paint we used to have."

His customer, a businessman from Roanoke would be smugly pleased to fly the Bellanca into Woodrum Field with that shiny new paint job.

In the south side of the hangar was a room, glass walled on three sides, which served as the pilot's lounge, the lunch room, reading room and communications facility to call the Automated Flight Service Station in Leesburg. The hangar sat approximately one hundred yards west of the runway and was in good shape, in spite of its many years of use. Chick automatically checked the refrigerator to see if any of the food would spoil while he was gone.

No waste, he thought as he saw only a jar of pickles on the second shelf.

November can show you every shade of gray just east of the Alleghany Mountains in Virginia. This particular November day was what Chick thought resembled battleship gray and it appeared that the ceiling was approximately five thousand feet. The visibility was probably fifteen miles, but there was a southwest wind a little gustier than comfortable. The temperature was in the mid-thirties.

He went out the door of the pilot's lounge and crossed a few steps through the yard to his trailer to finish packing a few personal things before he left for his sister's. As he threw a few things into a canvas bag, he turned on the television to listen to the news. He was not really surprised when the weather forecast called for snow flurries and a possible accumulation of two to four inches east of the mountains.

It looks like it will be a quiet weekend for the Chase City Airport, he thought. Then he went back through the pilot's lounge after locking his trailer and shut its door and left on a light and then slipped out though the now-silent hangar. He left the hangar doors closed but unlocked.

As his ancient Plymouth blinked its tail lights at the trailer as he touched the brakes going out the gravel road, the first snowflake fell on Chase City Runway 18.

*****

"Richmond Byrd Field information Sierra, 2255 Universal Coordinated Time, ceiling 3500 broken, 5000 overcast, visibility 8, temperature 35, dew point 28, barometric pressure 29.99, wind 230 degrees at 10, gusting 15, landing Runway 20, visual approach to Runway 20. Notice to Airmen: Runway end identifier lights Runway 33 out of service. Report you have information Sierra."

"Not too bad," said Rick to his wife Sara who was wearing the other pair of headsets.

"I think I'll check Leesburg Flight Service to see what the weather is like to the west."

Then without waiting for her reply, he reset the frequency for Leesburg Radio and said, "Leesburg Radio, Comanche 11345, listening on 122.1."

After a brief crackle, he heard: "Comanche 11345, Leesburg Radio, go ahead."

"Leesburg Radio, Comanche 11345 is twenty miles southwest of Lawrenceville VOR, VFR at 4,500 feet, squawking 1200, with Richmond Information Sierra, enroute to Charleston, West Virginia, requesting the Charlottesville, Roanoke, Lewisburg and Charleston Weather, please."

"Understood, 11345, stand by, please."

Seconds ticked by, then the Flight Service Station attendant keyed his mike again. "11345, the Charlottesville weather is 1500 overcast with blowing snow, temperature 31, dew point 30, wind 220 at 10 gusting to 15, visibility 3 miles. Roanoke weather is ceiling 1500, snow showers, temperature 32, dew point 30, wind 230 at 8, visibility 2 miles. Charleston, West

Virginia is 1000 overcast, visibility 4 miles, haze and light snow, temperature 33, dew point 31, wind 240 at 8. Over."

"Roger, Leesburg Radio, 11345 requests full weather briefing for the Appalachian area of Virginia."

"11345, a low pressure system in Southern Delaware with a cold front radiating from it southwesterly is causing a line of snow showers from Winston-Salem, North Carolina to Philadelphia. Accumulations in the last half hour are one half inch in Bluefield, West Virginia, and Ingalls Field at Hot Springs, Virginia. VFR westbound is not recommended."

"Roger, Leesburg, thank you very much, 11345."

"Oh fine, we won't make it to Charleston tonight," he said.

Then he said to Sara, "Did you hear that?"

Sara nodded and looked at him with questioning eyes.

He said to her over the intercom, "I really don't think we ought to go west any further. Let's look for a place to set down."

Sara had always been respectful of his attention to safety and had never been apprehensive to fly with Rick. This time both of them could see the slate gray in the west and she wasn't a bit disappointed when they decided not to continue any farther. But this was an area that neither of them knew well and they got out their charts to look for a landing site. On his IFR low altitude enroute chart Number 22, Rick noticed that the nearest airports were Brookneal, Chase City and Marks. Because Chase City had a non-directional beacon at the field, he chose it.

"Looks like Chase City," he said to her and she nodded to him as she looked up from her VFR Sectional Chart.

In the three years that she had been flying with him after he got his license, she had learned to read a Sectional Chart and to recognize the symbols for navigation radios, roads, railroads and rivers.

"It looks like there is an NDB on the field," she said.

"Yes," he said, "that's why I chose it."

"It really looks bad to the west," she said.

"Right," he said. Visibility was now dropping quickly and was around three miles.

"It looks like about ten miles to Chase City," he said.

"Let's tune the ADF."

And with that, he reached to the center of the panel. An additional hum began to come through the earphones which steadied in about ten seconds into a low faint crackle. As he twisted the dial, several other broadcasts were passed, but after some adjustment, he was able to find 342 Kilohertz for Chase City.

"Let's listen for the identifier," he said. Sara nodded and they both heard it at the same time, dah dit dah dit, da dit dit dah, dit.

"That's it," he said as the needle swung from its resting place at four o'clock to 11:30. "Since it's an uncontrolled field, we'll just go right straight for it until we see it and then enter the pattern and land."

She nodded without speaking.

"Sure is getting murky," he said. "I hope this doesn't get much worse, because if it does, I'm going to turn back."

"I'll keep watching for lights," she said

"You're a good sport, you know," he said, and squeezed her hand.

"Maybe we ought to drop down a bit," he said as he pulled the throttle back a bit. The plane began to descent through 3500 feet and the ADF needle swung straight up right at Chase City.

"It is snowing below us," he said.

"Do what you think is best, just don't push it," she said.

Now the snow was beginning to get thicker and the flakes were large. It became more difficult to see the ground. As they passed through 2500 feet, she said, "I see the four lane highway below."

"Good," he said. "Let's follow it to the field. It turns before the field, but it will help some."

"Okay," she said, and they both concentrated on the rising road as the plane descended through 2000 feet.

"I think we'll make it OK," he said.

"If this doesn't get worse at any greater rate than it's getting now, we'll be OK."

Now the identifier on the ADF was coming in clearly and there was no question that the Chase City NDB laid short mileage ahead of them.

"Leesburg Radio, Comanche 11345."

"11345, this is Leesburg Radio, go ahead."

"Comanche 11345 wishes to cancel our VFR flight plan. We are going to land due to weather at Chase City. We cannot maintain VFR."

"Roger that, 11345. Your VFR flight plan is cancelled as of eight past the hour. Do you need assistance?"

"Negative, Leesburg. We have positive identification of the NDB at Chase City and we are approximately eight miles east at 2000 feet."

"If you require assistance, please call."

"Thanks, Leesburg, we appreciate the help, 11345."

And then Rick twisted the dial of the radio to Unicom frequency. "Chase City Unicom, Chase City traffic, Comanche 11345, seven miles east, landing, requesting advisories."

Only a crackle filled their earphones. Rick waited approximately thirty seconds, then transmitted again.

"Chase City Unicom, Chase City traffic, Comanche 11345, six miles east at 2000 feet, entering the pattern left downwind for Runway 18."

Still no response.

"Let's get the lights on," he said to Sara as he began running through his landing check list. "Fuel on proper tank, electric fuel pump on, mixture to full rich, landing lights on."

They both began to look intently ahead for the Chase City beacon. Passing through 1500 feet, they thought it wouldn't be long before they saw it. The snow had thickened and visibility was down to approximately a mile and one half.

"Do you think we'll actually see the airport before we pass over it," she asked.

"Yes, I do," he said. "Unless it gets a lot worse, we should see it before we pass over it."

The needle never wavered as Rick carefully guided the Comanche toward the NDB. Both of them hoped to see some familiar pattern develop to insure that they were indeed at Chase City. With the needle firmly at the twelve o'clock position, they both knew that it wouldn't be long before they would see something. Then, out of the murky snow, about a mile ahead, they both saw the runway at the same time.

"There it is," they said together, as he turned the plane to the right to fall into a left downwind for Runway 18.

"Chase City traffic, Chase City traffic, Comanche 11435 is left downwind for Runway 18 at Chase City," he said.

Then to Sarah, he said, "Landing check list, mixture full rich, fuel on proper tank, electric fuel pump on, landing lights on, gear ready to come down."

As the speed bled off below 130 miles per hour, he tripped the gear switch and began watching for the green light to come on, indicating that the three landing gear legs were down. He always did this by putting his finger below the light and pushing on it, as if to make the gear come down, and when it did come on, he would call out to her, "Gear down," and would wait for one hundred twenty five miles per hour to put the first notch of flaps down.

As they passed through one twenty, he called out, "Flaps coming down one half," and then on the radio, "Chase City traffic, Comanche 11435 is left base for Runway 18 at Chase City." As they turned to final he called out again on the radio, "Chase City, Comanche 11435 is final for Runway 18 Chase City."

"Full flaps," he said, and watched as the vertical speed indicator settled on 800 feet per minute of descent.

"We'll be a little bit hot for this landing," he said, "but I think we'll be OK. There are 3900 feet of runway."

They passed the threshold indicating 95 miles per hour. By bleeding off the speed and waiting until it was at approximately 75 miles per hour, the Comanche chirped down to a safe landing and began its roll toward the south end of the field.

"According to the chart," he said, "the hangar is on the other end of the runway on the right."

"OK," she said, "I'll start looking. It shouldn't be hard to find."

He nodded with a smile because there would probably only be one hangar.

As they rolled up in front he stopped the Comanche in a spot away from the other two planes on the ramp and pulled the mixture. When the engine shuddered to a stop, he pushed the mixture back in, turned off the mag switch and the master switch, flipped off his headset and said to Sara, "If you'll get a coat on, we'll go call your parents."

"I think we should call them soon because the sooner they know we're not coming, the easier it will be for them," she said.

They each fell to their separate tasks in getting the plane post-flighted and ready for its night at Chase City. Once the control lock was in place, he squirmed out the door and joined Sara on the apron. The first flakes of the first snow were falling on their shoulders as they walked to the hangar.

"It looks like there a lounge or something there on the left," she said.

"Yes," he said. "Let's see if there is a phone."

They tried the door, but found it locked. As they turned to go around the building, he pointed out to her the squat Christmas tree looking structure and said, "That's the Chase City NDB. That's the radio that brought us in."

She looked and said, "Thanks, Chase City NDB and thank you, Starkeeper," as they turned around the corner of the hangar.

"Well, we're in luck, the door is unlocked," he said. He pulled the twenty foot tall hangar door aside to let her through.

"Gee, it's dark in here," she said.

"Wait a second till your eyes adjust, then we'll see what we can find," he said.

After a few seconds, they realized that the hangar was full of machinery: a tractor, a low wing airplane, a bi-plane over in the corner, partially dismantled, and a motorcycle sitting near them.

"That door over there has a light under it," she said.

They joined hands and walked through the machinery and vehicles to the door. It wasn't locked, and they stepped into the Chase City Pilot's Lounge.

*****

"9096 Papa, you can contact Washington Center now on 124.05."

"Roger, 96 Pop, good night."

"Center, 9096 Papa with you at Flight Level 240."

"Roger, 96 Papa, Roanoke altimeter two niner niner seven." Avery Langston glanced at his clipboard to confirm the next IFR intersection. Satisfied that he was still on course and would be approaching the intersection shortly, he again began scanning the instrument panel between long looks at the horizon.

"You know, I have a small confession to make," she said.

"And what's that?" he said.

"Well, for a long time when you used to go out with Daddy on those business trips and you all would take the company plane, I thought you and Daddy were riding as passengers and not flying the plane.'"

"For a time, I did ride in the front seat with him while he flew the plane, but I liked what I saw so much, I decided to learn to fly," he said.

"You know, it's strange to live with someone and not know that they're making such a big change in their life."

"Well, most of it happened when you were with the kids in Palm Beach and we weren't communicating much then. Life is full of little surprises, isn't it?"

"I just don't think I could ever learn what all those little gadgets and gizmos are for," she said.

"Well, it *is* a learning situation," he said. "After some time, you get used to it and it's almost like second nature."

"For instance," he said, "I've been timing these gas tanks since our takeoff and we are about ready to switch over to the other tanks."

"How much longer until we're there?" she asked.

"I'd say just a little less than two hours," he said.

"How many gas tanks does this thing have anyway?"

"Six,"he said. "We took off using the middle tank on each side or in each wing. We are now going to switch to the auxiliaries on the outboard end of each wing and we'll fly on them for an hour, then switch back to the inboard main tanks for landing in Nashville."

He reached between them to a pair of selector valves on the floor, gave them a pat and said, "Right here are the selectors where we switch from one tank to another. Since it's time to switch, I'll show you exactly how it's done."

He reached to the panel and flicked two switches upward for the electric fuel pumps and then moved both selector valves to the new tanks. After that, he watched the fuel pressure gauge on the right side of the panel as he switched the fuel pumps off to make sure that proper fuel pressure was maintained.

"I just can't get over how beautiful the sky is from twenty four thousand feet," she said. "I just don't think I'll ever get used to it."

"It's magnificent, isn't it," he said.

Then over a period of a few minutes, the purring growl of the engines began to sputter. Avery glanced to the right sharply at the tachometers and noticed that RPMs were dropping. Quickly he reached to the panel again and flicked on the electric fuel pumps.

"Something's wrong," he said.

Barbara, too stunned to speak, opened her mouth, but said nothing.

"Manifold pressure is dropping," he said. "We are losing power."

"What will we do?" she asked.

"Let's run the check list and make sure that we haven't missed something."

At that moment, what had been a sputter and a stutter became silence and the propellers began wind milling their way down to coasting speed. Avery pushed the thumb switch on his yoke, and said, "Washington Center, 9096 Papa has a problem."

Instantly Washington Center replied, "Roger, 96 Papa, what is the nature of your problem?"

"96 Papa has lost power on engines, passing through Flight Level 230 now, and declaring an emergency."

"96 Pop, say type aircraft, number of souls on board and hours of fuel on board."

"Center, 96 Pop has two souls on board, we are a PA31-350 with two hours thirty minutes fuel on board."

"Roger, 96 Pop, standby."

By this time, Avery was feverishly checking gauges, switches and valves in the cockpit, to make sure they were all in proper position, and finding all in order, he remained as perplexed as when the engines first began sputtering.

"Center, 96 Papa is going to have to make an emergency landing. Can you vector us to a nearby ILS airport?"

"96 Papa, standby," said Washington Center.

Long seconds passed. Then Center spoke though the headset. "96 Pop, the nearest ILS airport would be either Charlottesville or Richmond, both of which are sixty miles from your present position."

"Roger, Center, standby a second."

Then Avery said, "Center, can you vector 96 Papa to any airport within ten miles that has an instrument procedure?"

"96 Papa, standby a moment," said the center controller.

And then, without much of a further pause, he said, "The nearest airport to your position in your direction of travel is Chase City, Virginia, which has an NDB Runway 36 approach. The frequency of the NDB is 342 kilohertz, and according to latest notams, is properly in service."

"Roger, Center, 96 Papa understands Chase City, Virginia, NDB approach, Runway 36, frequency 342 kilohertz."

"Any theory on what the problem could be?"

"Negative, Center. 96 Papa has no idea what the problem is. We've lost power, no fire, all pressures are normal, the props are turning, but the pipes are not barking."

"Roger 96 Papa," said Center, "Say altitude."

"96 Papa is descending through 19,000 feet."

"Roger, 96 Papa," said Center.

"Avery, I'm really scared," said Barbara.

He looked at her and said, "I'm scared, too."

She said, "Well, do something. Are we going to have to go down through those clouds?"

"It sure looks like it," he said. "I'm, really sorry, honey, but I can't figure out what the problem is. Be sure and put your seat belt on tight. We'll do the best we can."

She nodded, as a tear started down her left cheek.

"Hand me that white booklet out of the glove box, please," he said.

"We are going to have to make an instrument approach into Chase City airport."

"Oh no," she said, "You know how I hate flying in the clouds."

"We don't have much choice this time," he said as he turned the ADF radio on and switched to the low frequency band. With the old style radio type of tuner, it took him a few seconds to get himself reoriented and he began listening for the identifier of Chase City.

Barbara opened the glove box in the panel. As it fell open, a plaque on the inside of the door became visible. "'Starkeeper' Piper Navajo PA31-350, serial number 31-00367, registered as N9096P, built especially for Paul Hargis by the Piper Aircraft Corporation, Lockhaven, Pennsylvania. June 12, 1972."

"Avery, I never saw that plaque before, what is it?" she asked.

"Your Dad named the plane for the Creator of the stars and the one who keeps them where they are. It's the Lord, honey," he said.

"Oh," she said. "We could use his help now, couldn't we?"

"Yes, we could," said Avery, then he keyed the mike and said, "Center, 96 Papa would like a vector to Chase City and our present distance."

"Roger, 96 Papa, turn right to a heading of 275 degrees, Chase City is twelve miles from your position."

"Roger, thank you, Center."

"96 Papa, are you still unable to figure out the problem?"

"Roger, Center, 96 Papa. Everything seems normal except for the fact that the engines are not producing any power. Center, should 96 Papa broadcast a Mayday?"

"Negative, 96 Papa, we have you in radar contact, but please squawk 7700."

Avery knew that the minute he turned the transponder to 7700, every radar scope receiving their transponder would light up with an alarm and their blip on the screen would glow brighter than the others.

"Avery, is there anything I can do?" asked Barbara.

"Just make sure that there aren't any loose articles around. Put all your books and stuff in the back seat and make sure your seat belt is good and tight."

"How soon before we go into the clouds?" she asked.

"About thirty seconds," he said, as he watched the puffy, white clouds rise toward the nose of the aircraft.

"Center, niner six papa would like the weather at Chase City"

"Niner six papa, stand by a moment, please.......niner six pop, the nearest weather station to Chase City is Roanoke. Roanoke weather is 1300 overcast, blowing snow, visibility two miles, temperature -1, dew point -1, wind 340 at 6. Lynchburg is 1000 overcast, visibility three miles, snow storm, temperature -1, dew point zero. Wind is 330 at five."

"Do you mean that there is snow in those clouds?" asked Barbara.

"Sure looks like it," said Avery.

"Better get the lights on before we go into the clouds," he said, thinking out loud. He flipped the switch to turn on the navigation lights and then turned off the strobe light.

"Center, niner six pop is on the gauges at 16,000 feet."

"Roger, niner six pop. Are you receiving Chase City yet?"

"Center, niner six pop is equipped with an old style ADF which we don't use very often. There is a lot of crackle on it, but I think I'm beginning to get an identifier."

"Roger, niner six pop. Keep center advised. Report receiving Chase City."

"Niner six pop, roger."

"Oh, honey, I'm so scared," Barbara said.

Avery looked at her for a moment and then said, "You know, any pilot that doesn't get scared once in while is a fool. But, we'll be alright, Barbara, just hang in there."

Then Avery turned his attention to the gauges, which now that they were enveloped in the silent mantle of snow, were his only sources of reference for up and down, left and right, forward and backward and height above sea level.

"Babs, hand me that low level enroute chart on your right, the one marked 22."

She handed it over to him. He handed it back to her quickly and said, "Please open it and see if you can find Roanoke on it."

"Center, 96 pop is passing through twelve thousand feet, still no power."

"Roger, 96 pop, there is no traffic between you and Chase City on radar. I will telephone Chase City on land line and tell them you are making an emergency landing."

"Thanks, Center. I sure wish I could figure out what the problem is."

"Have you tried switching fuel tanks?"

"Center, we had just switched to the outboard auxiliary tanks, maybe I should try that."

Avery moved the selectors from the aux tanks to the mains and made sure that the electric pumps were on. Long seconds passed as the snow swished past their windows.

Barbara noticed that there were times when she could not see the wingtips.

"Is this it, honey?" she asked as she handed him the chart.

"No. Roanoke has got to be way east of there. That's the part of the map that shows eastern Kentucky." He handed it quickly back to her and she began folding and unfolding it. Finally, she got it to where Roanoke showed up, and handed it to him.

"Let's see now, the elevation of the Chase City airport is 634. The NDB is on the field."

"What is an NDB?" she asked.

"Non-directional beacon," he said, "It's an old style navigation aid."

"Are we going to crash, Avery?" she asked, visibly shaking.

"No, honey, just relax now. This is going to be a little tight, but I think we will make it OK. This is a good old plane, the autopilot will keep us right side up and the ADF is working good."

He glanced toward the radio. With his right hand, he made a small adjustment to the tuning knob and noticed that the pointer on the indicator came alive for the first time.

"Listen carefully," he said and turned the volume up so they both could hear.

"What are you listening for?" she asked.

"The Morse code identifier," he said. "Every NDB has an identifier so that you can tell you are on the right frequency."

"I wouldn't know what to listen for," she said.

"Well, it's a series of dots and dashes. You just kinda have to know that to listen for."

"Do you think you have the right one?" she asked.

"Well, I'm pretty sure of it, but in another minute or two, we should be positive."

He keyed the microphone and said, "Center, 96 pop is passing through niner thousand feet, still no power."

"Roger, 96 pop," said Center.

Just then the right engine sputtered a little and immediately then the left engine sputtered. It was the first sign of life either engine had shown since 23,000 feet.

"Oh," she said. "Do you think the engines are going to work?"

"Well, we'll see. Let's just give them a little more time. It could be a blocked fuel line or something like that."

The engines kept sputtering and spurting, stuttering and popping, but didn't produce any power. Avery adjusted the propeller pitch controls to bring the RPMs up to maximum, hoping that would bring further signs of life to the freely rotating engines.

"Hand me that booklet over there, please," he asked. "I'd better look at the instrument approach procedure for Chase City."

"Is it terribly complicated?" she asked.

"I don't know," he said. "Let me read through it first." He found the chart he wanted, folded the booklet and clipped it to the yoke.

"See this little spot?" he asked. "That's the Chase City NDB."

"Well, it's right beside the runway," she said.

"Right," he said. "We won't have a long approach to shoot." With that, he reached for the ADF dial and moved it a bit. The Morse code identifier for the first time came through clearly.

"That's Chase City," he said. "Now I'm sure we are on the right frequency."

The ADF indicator needle began turning obediently from a four o'clock position toward twelve o'clock.

"When the needle points straight up, the NDB is directly in front of the airplane."

"Center, niner six pop is receiving Chase City NDB."

"Roger, niner six pop. Center is still trying to reach Chase City on land line. No answer."

"Niner six pop is passing through six thousand feet."

"Roger, niner six pop."

Then, "Niner six pop, Center is in contact with personnel at Chase City. Told them you are executing an emergency approach and landing. There is no equipment there, but they say the runway is clear. They do have snow, estimated ceiling one thousand feet, visibility is estimated two miles, light wind from the northwest. Over."

"Roger, niner six pop."

"OK, honey, I am going to tell you how we do this as we do it. That will keep me sharper and it'll tell you exactly what I'm doing all the time. I'm just going to talk as I think. OK, let's see, landing check list: fuel on proper tank, electric fuel pumps on, mixture to full rich, alternate air source on, we'll turn on the landing lights when we are in the clear. OK we're ready to drop the landing gear."

"When will you do that?" she asked.

"Once we are inbound on the approach," he said. "What we'll do is cross over the NDB from the southeast, loop around to the right, and pass over the NDB again, and then fly south a bit, make a procedure turn like it shows on this approach plate, and turn inbound to land, without dropping below one thousand two hundred feet."

"Where are we in relation to the field now?" she asked.

"Center, niner six pop needs to know course and distance to Chase City."

"Niner six pop, Chase City is one o'clock and five miles."

"Roger, niner six pop."

Now the identifier became the loudest sound in the cockpit. With the engines occasionally sputtering and the whistling of the wind, their attention was riveted to the gauges on the panel and the identifier in their ears.

"I think we are pretty close," he said, as he glanced at her momentarily. She just nodded, gritted her teeth and gave his knee a squeeze. He could tell she was very frightened.

"It's going to be alright. Starkeeper is watching over us."

"Those instructors wore us out on these NDB approaches when I was taking my instrument training.

We've got a good signal from the NDB and I think we're going to be alright."

She nodded and gave a sob at the same time and gave his knee another squeeze. Just as he looked at the ADF, the needle swung from twelve o'clock to six o'clock.

"There it is," he said. "We've just passed over the NDB, now to make our tear drop turn to the right."

"Center, niner six pop, has just passed the Chase City NDB, on the approach now."

"Roger, Center clears niner six pop for the Runway 36 NDB approach at Chase City. Switch to Unicom, 122.8 is approved, call us on land line after you land. Good luck."

"'Roger, Center, thanks, niner six pop."

Avery twisted the dial on the navcom radio to 122.8 and called, "Chase City Unicom, Chase City Unicom, Navajo niner zero niner six papa, overhead, passing through four thousand, emergency landing, engines out, requesting advisories, over."

No reply from the Unicom.

Then all of a sudden, "Navajo niner zero niner six papa, this is Chase City Unicom, transient pilot transmitting, no regular personnel here. We have a little bit of snow on the runway, light wind from the northwest, no other traffic, all the lights are on. Over."

"Thanks, Chase City. We have our hands full here, passing through four thousand now, niner six pop."

"Roger, niner six pop, can hear you but cannot see you. Good luck."

"Thanks, niner six pop."

By now they had completed their teardrop turn to the right and were heading back over the NDB.

"Watch our course," he said. "We should be on 180."

The ADF needle moved from close to 12 o'clock to six o'clock again as they passed over the NDB southbound.

"Where are we now?" she asked.

"Just passing over the field, outbound on a heading of 180," he said. "Now we'll fly outbound for two minutes and make our procedure turn inbound and look for the airport."

"How high are we?"

"Three thousand five hundred feet," he said. "I'm not going to drop the landing gear until I see the field lights."

Their airspeed was now one hundred thirty knots. Long seconds ticked by. They flew the outbound course, then he said, "I'm not going to fly a full two minutes outbound, we will turn inbound sooner."

"What does that mean?" she asked.

"Well, we're going to have to make some adjustments," he said.

"Wait a minute."

"We'll fly inbound for one minute forty five seconds and if we don't see the field, we're going to have to land somewhere else."

"Oh, my God," she said.

Now they were making a gentle turn to the left, then to the right and Barbara watched as the ADF needle went to seven o'clock, then six o'clock, then five o'clock, four o'clock, three o'clock, two o'clock and then seemed to hold about one thirty o'clock. With another gentle turn, Avery brought the Navajo around to where the needle stood straight up.

"Watch our altitude carefully," he said. "If it gets below one thousand feet, let me know."

He knew that he wouldn't let it get below twelve hundred feet, but he wanted to give her something to do so she wouldn't be so frightened.

"Do you see anything ahead?" he asked.

"No," she said. "It's just all snow."

"Well, it's right at dark," he said. "I would expect we'll be able to see those lights pretty soon."

"What if we don't break out in time?" she asked.

He didn't answer her and just kept looking at the dials. Twenty seconds.

"We should be seeing the field any time now," he said.

Still the snow whistled around them.

"I see a light," she said. "I see a light."

With that, Avery tripped the gear lever and the landing gear began to come down.

"There it is," he said. "Boy, a landing strip never looked so good. We are a bit high, so hang on tight."

"OK, honey."

The Navajo decelerated more quickly than he expected. Dropping the gear and the flaps at the same time slowed them to one hundred knots. Now the Navajo descended quickly toward the black ribbon ahead of them in the snow.

"I guess what I saw was the little flashing light to the left," she said.

"That's the beacon," he said.

"Look for the runway lights."

Just as he spoke, they were both able to see the tiny flickers of light on each side of the blacktop.

"Still no power," he said. "We may touch down a little bit hard, but I think we're OK."

"OK," she said.

"A little firmer than normal, but thank you Starkeeper for this little runway," he thought, as the plane rolled toward the far end of the runway.

At first he thought he was going to be able to decelerate the plane well with the brakes, but as he got further down the runway, it seemed to get more slippery.

"I think we may have a little trouble stopping by the end of the runway," he said, and at that point, both of the main tires locked on the snow. The Navajo began a graceful slew to the right but then just as gracefully slewed to the left, and just as they rolled to a stop, the nose wheel went off the end of the runway onto a small gravel patch.

"Whooee," he said. "That was close." They both just sat there for a minute, noticing for the first time that the propellers had stopped somewhere during the landing. The loudest sound at this point was the Chase City NDB in the speaker phones.

"Dah dit dah dit, dah dit dit dah, dit," it repeated over and over, as they sat there drinking in their survival.

When he was finally able to do so, Avery began turning things off, and then he spoke to Barbara.

"Close, but we made it. Let's get to a phone to call Center and tell them we're OK."

"You did good, Avery. You saved us both."

"There isn't a life on this earth I'd rather save than yours," he said. Then he reached over and opened the door so they could get out. A gust of wind caught the door and blew the cabin full of snowflakes as they stepped out.

"It sure feels good, doesn't it?" he laughed, and she noticed for the first time that he was smiling.

"I'll get the bags," he said. As he opened the hatch door, he could hear someone running toward them.

"You folks had a close call. Is everybody OK?" asked Rick.

"Well, yes," they both answered together.

"Welcome to Chase City," Rick said. "We've only been here about fifteen minutes ourselves," he said. "I could hear you pass overhead," he said, "even though your engines weren't running. Let's get you all inside, out of this snow."

The three of them started back up the runway toward the hangar. They walked into the same hangar that Rick and Sara had walked through just a few minutes before, and then stepped into the pilots' lounge. As they stepped in, Sara, who had been checking the stove and refrigerator, turned and came over to them to be introduced.

Avery said, "My name is Avery Langston and this is my wife, Barbara. We're mighty glad to have your help and assistance tonight."

"I'm Rick Jones and this is my wife, Sara," he said. "We landed here just a few minutes ago in that Comanche out on the ramp. Looks like the weather has prevented a lot of holiday happiness this time"

"Well, I don't think the weather had anything to do with our problem," said Avery. "We were cruising along serenely at twenty four thousand when we lost power and had to come down into this weather."

"Did you shoot the whole approach dead stick?" asked Rick.

"Yes, and I think my knees are going to be trembling for a week," said Avery.

Barbara said, "Well, you could have fooled me."

"It doesn't mean that I wasn't scared. We were just lucky not to have run off the other end of the runway with that snow on it."

"It just shows you how fast some things can happen. When we landed just twenty minutes ago, there was no snow on the runway."

"Boy, I'm hungry. Is there anything to eat?" said Rick.

"Sure," said Sara. "We've got our snacks and the other stuff for the holidays. Since we're not going to be there for dinner, I guess I could put the turkey in the oven and warm it up. Do you folks think you could eat a little turkey dinner?"

Unanimous grins made the answer obvious.

Rick said to Avery, "Why don't we take that old Plymouth there and go down the runway and tow your plane up by the hangar? Maybe we can figure out what the problem is."

"I'd go for that," said Avery.

The two men went out and climbed into the old Plymouth. By rigging a rope to the tail tie down loop, they pulled the Navajo back up the runway to the hangar area.

"Boy, that's a lot better," said Avery. "I feel better about leaving the plane here than down there at the end of the runway."

Avery found a check cup in the hangar and went to the right outboard auxiliary tank drain under the wing and drained a few ounces to see if water or any other contamination were present. The clear liquid did not show any contamination, but when Avery sniffed it, the distinct aroma of kerosene made him exclaim out loud to Rick, "It's jet fuel, it's jet fuel. That's what the problem was. I'll never turn my back on a line boy again."

"Well," said Rick, "from a repair standpoint, you may be in luck. Once we purge the lines and drain those tanks and clean the spark plugs, you may find that there is no real damage to the plane."

"That would be terrific," said Avery. "I bought this old Navajo from my father in law and he bought it new. It has been a good old plane and I've grown attached to it."

"Well, let's leave that job for the morning and go get some dinner."

"Thank goodness, it doesn't take as long for a turkey to heat up as it does to cook it originally," said Sara. "I think we can have a good dinner here in about twenty minutes more."

"There's a head of lettuce in the refrigerator. Why don't we make a salad?" asked Barbara.

"Good idea. This may turn out to be a holiday treat after all," said Sara.

"Where were you going?" asked Barbara.

"We were on our way to my parents for the holidays in Charleston," answered Sara.

As they came in the door, Avery was saying to Rick, "I just couldn't figure it out. About five minutes after we switched tanks, the engines started stumbling and then went completely dead. And even though I switched tanks back to the inboard mains, we were not able to get anything to restart."

"Maybe the sparkplugs were fouled with the jet fuel," said Rick.

"We can check that after a while."

As they gathered at the dinner table, a park bench painted white, with the luggage now moved off of it, Sara brought the steaming turkey.

"Where is this place, anyhow?" Barbara asked Avery.

Avery pointed his thumb at the chart on the wall behind him and said, "Chase City, Virginia, CXE. We are approximately sixty five miles east southeast of Roanoke. It looks like the people who work here have left for the holidays."

Rick said, "We are new here ourselves. We've never landed here before and the field was totally deserted when we landed."

"It looks like somebody keeps this place pretty busy, though, with all the painting work that's being done in the hangar," said Avery.

"Yes, that's sure a nice job on that Bellanca Viking."

"What's that out the window?" asked Barbara, indicating with her chin.

"That, my dear, is what got us here safely. That's the Chase City NDB."

"Looks like an old one, too," he added.

"The fellow that taught me how to fly told me that most of the NDB's that are shaped like that were built in the thirties," he added.

"Girls," he said turning to them. "That little radio saved our bacon tonight."

And with that, he raised his glass in a mock solemnity and said, "Thank you, Starkeeper, for bringing us all home safely tonight and thank you, Chase City NDB, long may your kilohertz wave."

Just outside in the snow, the old NDB acknowledged the toast the same way it had since 1937. "Dah dit dah dit. Dah dit dit dah. Dit."

8

TANGIER ISLAND

A telephone that wakes you up in the middle of the night is one thing. But when you are awakened by a knock at the door, it's different. With the call, you can deal with someone who is far away or at least not in your face. With a knock at the door, someone is there, someone who has to be dealt with. Is it dangerous? Is it a mistake? You don't just go fling the door open, especially if you have been asleep for three hours, you are still tired, your sweet wife is asleep in the bed next to you, you are in a motel room in a new place, unfamiliar, and you have no weapon.

Still, the knock was soft, not belligerent, almost pleading, not demanding. Kevin got out of bed as softly as he could, turned on the light in the closet, familiarized himself with the layout of the room, and approached the door. He looked through the peep hole. It was the lady who had checked them in before supper. With her was an older man with a brown suede jacket and a small gold badge.

"What is it?" Kevin asked.

"Mr. Gallagher, it's Mrs. Holton. We need some help."

Kevin opened the door.

"What is it?" He asked a second time.

"There has been an accident. Mrs. Acosta, the pregnant lady who sat across from you all at supper has fallen off the porch. She is unconscious. Her husband is frantic. We called the Emergency Room at the clinic at Havre de Grace. Based on what we told the Doctor on duty, he thinks she may have some kind of a hematoma, I think he called it. The doctor says it is an emergency and to get her to the hospital at the University of Maryland in College Park as soon as we can. He said he would alert them and have an ambulance standing by to take her. I know it's a big imposition, but could you fly her there?"

"Wow," said Kevin, as he stepped into the lighted hall.

"First of all, where is she?"

"Downstairs in room 110. You have the only aircraft on the island, all the other tourists left after dinner. If we can't fly her out, she may not make it. The longer she goes, the less chance that the baby will survive or be normal."

The last of the cobwebs of sleep had left him. Sure, his plane was ready, enough fuel to make the trip, but what about the weather? It looked low when they walked outside after dinner.

"I'll dress," he said.

"Thank you," she said. She and the constable started off down the hall.

He gently woke his wife and told her about the situation.

"We may be her only chance," he said. "No one else is here with an airplane. Do you want to go with me?"

"Let me dress, I'll think about it. Where is she?"

"Downstairs, room one ten. Leave our stuff in the room. We'll come back before we go home."

"OK," she said, "see you down there as soon as I can dress."

Mrs. Acosta was pale. She looked thin for a woman eight months pregnant. Her husband was holding her hand and sobbing when Kevin came in. Mrs. Holton introduced Kevin to Mr. Acosta.

"Thank you," was all he could choke out.

"I have a station wagon in the parking lot," said the constable. "We can ride in it and take her to the airport that way."

It was only about four tenths of a mile to the airport, just a leisurely walk for the able, but this lady was unconscious and her condition was deteriorating by the minute.

"Let's get her to the plane as quickly as we can," he said.

Just then Sheila, his wife, came to the door. When she saw him, she came to his side. The five of them gathered up the edges of the blanket she lay on and lifted her. No response from her. Luckily, they were on the first floor. Only six steps separated them from ground level. Carefully, they eased down the hall and out the door at the end. The station wagon was a 1957 Ford, Kevin recognized the year immediately. Out here on the island, people keep their machinery a long time, he thought.

After Constable Bell lowered the back door and threw out the cardboard box of fishnet and some other junk, they passed her in, keeping a pillow under her head.

"At which airport is the ambulance?" asked Kevin.

"Washington National, at Butler Aviation," answered Bell.

Sandy Acosta looked to be about thirty. Her husband, not much older. He looked scared.

"Do you have any medical experience, Mr. Acosta?"

"Call me Sid, Mr. Gallagher. No, I am an accountant. This was our last planned outing before the baby. Sheila and I have been coming here for the peace and quiet for years each summer. She thought we could do it again this year OK. All I know is that she is the most important person in the world. What can I do to help?"

"For now, just stand by. We need to decide who will go along. We have four seats. You and your wife will be in the back. Sheila, do you want to go?"

"Yes, I'll go. I was kinda hoping you would locate someone with medical experience, though."

"This will be a short flight, we haven't a moment to loose. I need five minutes to look at the charts, then I will help you complete the preflight. Will you untie the ropes?"

"Sure," she said.

He ran to the cowling and opened the hatch to check the oil. Plenty and clean, too. He smiled. Good machine. He grabbed his Washington Sectional from above the panel. Five minutes to plan a night flight, under a low ceiling, visibility about eight, no visual checkpoints, then down the Anacostia River into a major international airport, wow!

Carefully, they eased her into her husband's arms in the back seat. At Kevin's instruction, Sid was already seated and belted in. He gently put the shoulder harness around Mrs. Acosta.

"Better leave off the seatbelt," Kevin said. "In her condition, it would do more damage than good."

"I agree," said Mr. Acosta.

Sheila climbed into her seat and strapped in. They had two flashlights. No runway lights graced the grass field. How was he to be sure he was straight down the runway?

"You see that church steeple down there?" said Bell.

"Yes," said Kevin.

"Come over here," said Bell and the two walked the fifty yards to the south end of the runway.

"From this end, that church steeple is the best landmark. From here, the runway lies just between that and that group of trees to the right."

"Thanks," said Kevin, "anything else?"

"Yes, it's soft just beyond half way, best be off the ground by then."

"How soft?" Asked Kevin.

"There was water standing in the area this evening from that shower this afternoon. It may be gone by now, but if it is not, that area will be soggy, not to mention, maybe under three or so inches of water."

"You are right, I don't want to hit that. Anything else?"

"Yes, with these low clouds, you will have to hug the deck. I doubt if you can get above two hundred feet. Watch for the bay bridge over to Annapolis. Remember, port for red and green for starboard. There are marking lights about fifty feet above the water line and a white light at the bottom and top center of the bridge."

"How many piers?" asked Kevin.

"Plenty, best you go between the middle two. They are about five hundred feet apart."

"Thanks," said Kevin.

"Good luck, young fellow. You are going to need it. If it weren't for you and this airplane, I think she would not last until we could get her to a hospital."

They quickly strode back to the 182.

"Clear," he said, not really loudly. The starter smoothly turned the big two bladed prop. It caught on the fifth blade and settled into a rumble.

"How much ceiling will we have?" Sheila asked.

"Maybe three hundred feet," said Kevin.

"How do you plan to go? What can I do?"

"We'll take off to the north, turn left to a heading of three two zero and fly toward shore. There is a bridge just before landfall. We may need to fly under it. The piers are five hundred feet apart, well lit, but only a hundred feet above sea level. We need to be down at that level well before the bridge. Let's see, fuel on both, both magnetos on, trim set, flaps set on two notches, directional gyro set with the compass at zero two zero degrees, altimeter set at six feet above sea level, door latched. Let's get your door."

"I intend to call an emergency on 121.5 as soon as we are aloft. Then we will try Washington Center. I hope we can raise someone. Set the transponder to seventy seven hundred."

She turned the four dials. There was no return wink from the transponder, just its steady "On" light.

"You ready?" he asked Mr. Acosta. Acosta nodded grimly.

Kevin brought the throttle up to full RPM, holding the brakes. Landing lights on. He released the brakes. The big plane surged ahead, blowing dew off of the midnight grass. All he could see through the windshield was grass. Keep your heading straight with the directional gyro, just like IFR training. At fifty miles per hour, he put back pressure on the yoke. In a few seconds 5611 B leaped out of the grass, spraying dew and grass cuttings. Hold heading and attitude. Stabilize airspeed at eighty. Altitude now one hundred. Careful, don't punch into the clouds. He milked off the flaps and nosed over at one hundred fifty feet MSL.

"Good enough, but boy is it black. Wow, night IFR couldn't be any more challenging than this," he thought.

With no ground references ahead of them, he began a one half standard rate turn to the left. The sleeping village of Tangier came into sight, a few lights still on at three AM.

"OK, heading two two zero, altitude one fifty, airspeed coming up to one forty, trim for cruise. Landing light off."

"How long to the bridge? "Sheila asked.

"About twenty two minutes," Kevin said.

"Do you think you should call?" she whispered into the intercom.

"His eye is on the sparrow, and I know He watches me," said Kevin. "Here we are, Starkeeper, yours for another night. Hold us tight."

No one spoke for a while.

"I'd better try the radio," he said, "Pan, pan, pan, Cessna Skylane five six one one bravo, off Tangier Island, with a medical emergency, pan, pan, pan." Seconds passed. No response.

"Pan, pan, pan, Cessna Skylane five six one one bravo, off Tangier Island, with a medical emergency, pan, pan, pan."

"I say, Skylane five six one one bravo, this is Concorde Golf Bravo Oscar Alpha Golf, we read you, can we assist?"

"Thanks Alpha Golf, Five Six One One Bravo is flying a medical patient to Washington National for emergency medical treatment. I guess no one else can hear me. We estimate National in forty minutes, we cannot raise Washington Approach yet, will you call and alert them? We are squawking seventy seven hundred."

"Roger, wilco, five six one one bravo, we are talking to Washington Approach on another frequency and will lose contact with you shortly. What frequency do you intend to call Washington Approach on?"

"We will call on 128.85 starting in about ten minutes. We are cruising at one hundred fifty feet to avoid IFR above. Tell them we expect to fly up the Anacostia River to the field."

"Roger, five six one one bravo, Concorde Alpha Golf standing by."

"What a great break, those guys are heading for Dulles and are already talking to Washington Approach."

"Do you think they will let us into their airspace," Sheila asked.

"Good question, let's just keep on going and they will tell us."

"I see a red and green light ahead," she said.

"Oh, boy, that's the bay bridge. We need to get our altitude down to one hundred. Stay with me as we approach and go through. Hold the yoke with me. Don't let the plane go up any. We need to be below one hundred to be safe."

"Safe, you call this safe?" she said.

"The Starkeeper is watching out for us," Kevin said softly.

"Oh me, of little faith," she said sarcastically.

He smiled, she smiled, then they looked ahead at the looming bridge, just its pillars sticking out of the black water and into the dark gray above.

It seemed like a ride at the circus. They shot through almost exactly in the middle between the red and green lights.

"Whew, now what?" she asked.

"Let's tune the marine beacon on 563. It's located almost directly on our flight path, just a little to the left. Once we pass it, we should be able to get the Annapolis VOR."

He was glad he hadn't taken the old ADF radio out. Even though they had a new hand held GPS, it was reassuring to have as much information as possible.

Just as they shot over the marine buoy, Kevin called, "Washington Center, Cessna five six one one bravo." No answer.

"Kevin, Sandy's breathing has changed," called Sid from the back seat. "It's slower and deeper, she seems to be trying harder. How much longer?"

"About twenty minutes," he said to Sid.

"Hurry, Lord," said Sid.

"Washington Center, Washington Center, Skyline five six one one bravo." Still no answer.

"Let's try Washington Approach," he said, turning the dial as he spoke. "Washington Approach, Skyline five six one one bravo."

"Five six one one bravo, Washington Approach, confirm squawking seven seven zero zero."

"That is affirmative, Five six one one bravo is squawking seventy seven hundred."

"Say intentions, five six one one bravo, we understand an ambulance is waiting for you at Butler."

"Roger, Approach. Five six one one bravo is level at one hundred fifty feet, airspeed one hundred thirty knots. We intend to fly up the Anacostia River to the field."

"Understood, five six one one bravo. Are you aware that there are six bridges across the Anacostia River between you and the field?"

"We are now, Approach. Any advice?"

"Yes, Metropolitan Police cruisers will be on the center span of each bridge with all lights on to help you. Say flight conditions."

"Good VFR, ceiling three hundred estimated, visibility six miles, no turbulence."

"I guess you have enough turbulence on board tonight, don't you five six one one bravo?"

"That's affirmative. How far do you make it to the first bridge?"

"Seven miles. We have you now in radar contact, you can switch squawks to seven zero one one."

"I see the first bridge," said Sheila and she pointed ahead.

"No problem with clearance, that one is low," said Kevin. Now they could see three bridges, or rather, they could see the flashing lights of police cruisers. As they whisked over the first bridge, Kevin and Sheila could see a television crew with its camera pointed at them.

The next bridge had a few cars stopped in addition to the police cruiser. By the time they got over the last bridge, there must have been fifty people waving them on.

"Caution, five six one one bravo, the river makes a left turn of about forty degrees about two miles ahead. Report entering the turn."

"Roger, Approach."

"And five six one one bravo, call tower now on one one eight decimal niner."

"Roger, Approach, thanks, five six one one bravo."

"Washington National Tower, Cessna five six one one bravo."

"Five six one one bravo, Washington Tower, plan on straight in to runway two three, show us your landing light, please."

"Roger, Tower, five six one one bravo."

Out of the murk, Washington National appeared, one of the great airports of the world and only three miles away they could not see it. Now it filled the windshield with red, green, blue, yellow and white lights, flashing, glowing, blinking. What a sight.

He pulled back the throttle and in a few seconds pulled on a notch of flaps. He could see the two and the three on the runway now.

"Five six one one bravo has runway two three," he said.

"Cleared to land, five six one one bravo," said Tower.

"After landing, taxi to Butler via taxiway golf. You should see the flashing lights to your left as you land."

"Thanks, Tower, we are glad to see you tonight."

"Good luck with your passenger."

The wheels yipped as he swept the 182 onto Runway two three. A quick taxi to Butler, a quick handshake from Sid, and they were gone. He and Sheila stood alone next to the plane, listening to it cool.

They slept in the pilot's lounge until noon, curled up like spoons in the recliner.

9

RAMPARTS

The sound of voices in the next room woke John. He quickly put sense of place and time back together. Huntington, West Virginia, airport pilot's lounge, middle of the night, asleep in a lounger. It must be the middle of the night. Dim light was showing under the door in the hall.

"Brothers, am glad to see you." Thick accent. Sounded middle eastern.

"Quickly now, must tell you. Rahman says device obtained from man in Russian navy at Sevastopol. Small device, six kilotons. Total destruction within one kilometer. Is concealed in radome under wing. Red handle taped to top of cockpit runs through wing to pins holding radome on wing. Pull handle, device drops. Armed when dropped. Drop if you can. If not, fly into target. Good luck. Allah ackbar!"

"Am I dreaming? These guys are terrorists! Who or what do they intend to destroy with that 'device'?"

Now wide awake, he hoped they did not hear him. He sneaked to the window and looked through the opening into the night. On the ramp nearby was a Cessna 210, complete with radar pod under the right wing. Three men talked briefly, then embraced. One walked around the terminal building into the darkness. The other two got into the 210. In a bit, the prop started to turn, then the engine caught.

He looked up at the tower, now dark and closed until seven A.M. No chance those guys are going to file a flight plan. I wonder where they are heading with that thing? As the plane started to taxi out to the runway, he went to the pay phone on the wall. No dial tone. He jiggled the handle. No go, still no dial tone.

Now what? His bag was beside the lounger he had slept in. When he got back to the airport, he was simply exhausted, "brain dead," as one of his friends called it. The Deposition of Rollo Norton had taken most of the afternoon and into the evening. It was black dark when he walked to his rental car to go to the airport. He was clearly too tired to fly, but he decided to get dinner at Renaldo's and sleep in the pilot's lounge rather than get a motel room. The clock on the wall read four thirty. Next to the clock was the calendar for January.

What is today, anyway? He thought. January 20. My brother's birthday. Have to give him a call later, to follow up the card already sent."

"Holy cow! Today is Inauguration Day."

Quickly he gathered up his bag and ran from the building toward his airplane. Got to keep those guys in sight! Already, the 210 was at the threshold of the runway. Now he could hear the sound of the propeller as its tips approached the sound barrier. What a scream!

He ran across the darkened tarmac to his Aztec. Straight to the tie downs. No time to preflight, sort things out in the air. All lines clear, no obvious problems with hangar rash or damage, he thought as he leaped onto the right wing and tried to find the lock with his key. It was about thirty five degrees, and a clear starry night. Too bad he had no time to stop and enjoy it.

Lurching into the pilot's seat, he flipped on the master switch, and as soon as he could, pushed the starter switch forward for the left engine. He didn't have time to prime it, and it went six blades before it caught. He immediately cranked the right engine. No lights, he thought. Don't want them to see me.

As the 210 climbed into the night, he thought it would be very difficult to follow. But, follow he must, anyway.

He checked the magnetos on the roll to the runway, scrambling to get his headset on and make some semblance of order out of his departure. Without slowing down, he taxied quickly onto Runway 12 and brought the power up slowly on both sides. No hesitation. The book says it is safe to take off as soon as the engines will come up to full power without hesitation. Now rolling, now light on the wheels, now airborne, the Aztec hauled itself into the night.

"Starkeeper, I need your help tonight," he prayed. "Climb, baby. Get us some altitude to make the radio reach out. Who would be the nearest soul he could contact at this hour?"

He could make out the shape of the 210 about five or six miles ahead, no lights, at about three thousand feet.

Just about the same speed, he thought, and he leveled off at three thousand in trail. Not enough altitude yet to call Indy Center. Charleston Approach would be the nearest. From memory, he thumbed the upper com radio to 124.1.

"Charleston Approach, Aztec five six one one bravo." Silence. Still too far and too low for Charleston.

He tried the emergency frequency 121.5. No response. Minutes passed. He could see the neighborhood where Pat and Courtney would be asleep. Sweet kids, he thought. The Huntington Mall passed below and Ona Airpark. "How do I get myself into these things?"

Try Charleston again. "Charleston Approach, Aztec five six one one bravo." Just the crackle of normal background noise in the headset, then "Aztec five six one one bravo, Charleston Approach." Sleepy voice.

"Glad you are with me, Charleston Approach, five six one one bravo is off Huntington Tri-State with an emergency not involving the aircraft or pilot."

"Five six one one bravo, squawk 7700 and ident. What is the nature of your emergency?"

"Five six one one bravo overheard three middle eastern men on the ground at Huntington talking about what seems a plan to commit a terrorist act. Can you patch me through to someone who can help? I am following their Cessna 210 at three thousand feet, lights off. I can just barely keep up with them. If they spot me and try to outrun me, I think they can, especially if their plane is turbocharged. I don't believe they have seen me. I took off about two minutes behind them. They definitely didn't know I was there when they were talking. Is the FBI reachable by land line? Who else is there?"

"Stand by, five six one one bravo."

Long silence. The green light on the transponder showed "7700" in its windows.

"Wow, every radar that could receive him would be lit up and bells ringing."

"Five six one one bravo, squawk 4444 now."

He turned the dials quickly.

"Five six one one bravo, I have talked to Major Gallagher over at the National Guard Hangar. He and his men have been out on a night mission. Call him on 123.45. We will stand by. Call us back when you decide what to do."

"Roger, Charleston, five six one one bravo."

What luck, Kevin is at the National Guard Hangar! John immediately tuned the number one com to 123.45, the helicopter frequency usually used by the National Guard, and kept 124.1 on the number two.

"National Guard, November five six one one bravo, calling on 123.45."

"Five six one one bravo, this is Major Gallagher of the West Virginia National Guard. Identify yourself, please."

"Kevin, this is John Hache, five six one one bravo."

"What are you doing up at this hour of the night, John?"

"I was asleep in the pilots lounge at TriState when these guys ahead of me in the 210 woke me up talking in the hall just outside my door. How much did Charleston Approach tell you?"

"That you are an Aztec following a Cessna 210 with two middle eastern men on board who you believe are up to some kind of terrorist play. What do you think they are up to, John?"

"Kevin, it's January 20. What does that mean to you? These guys have a device in the radome under the right wing. The other man said that they obtained it in Sevastopol from a man in the Russian navy. Sounds like some kind of black market deal to get a nuclear device. One said it was only six kilotons, and could wipe out a kilometer wide area."

"Where are you now, John?"

"If you look out the window, you could see me if I had my running lights on. I am about three miles off of the south end of runway 23, one hundred sixty knots, level at two thousand feet."

"I am calling the Adjutant General, stand by but keep following those guys."

"Roger," said John, "standing by."

In a minute, came another voice.

"November five six one one bravo, this is General Miller. Are you Beulah's son?"

"Affirmative, Bill, long time no see."

"John, Kevin is in a Guard C130, but they have a problem with the number two engine. He has your old buddy Mike Mealey with him as loadmaster and copilot. They are the only two aboard. Others will follow in other aircraft later. I agree with you this is a very dangerous situation. Those guys scare me the longer they head east. Do you know what day this is?"

"Affirmative, Bill, what do you want me to do?"

"Keep following them until we catch up. We have scrambled jets from Pax River and Wright Field in Dayton. They are at least half an hour away. Where are you now?"

"Five six one one bravo is passing the Dupont Plant at Belle. These guys seem to be following the river for now. They are right at the same height as the hills on either side."

"Five six one one bravo, this is National Guard 465."

"Kevin, I hear you loud and clear, how me?"

"Five by five. We are going to have to abort. Our number two engine is running way too hot, we are returning to Charley West."

The wind whistled around the Aztec and the earphones hummed their little background noises. He checked around the cockpit for the first time since taking off. His scarf was partly caught in the door and was trailing about six inches along the second window. Otherwise, except for just being thrown into the plane, everything was in order. He looked at the fuel gauges, then turned the tank selectors on each side. He was low on fuel, probably two hours worth, maybe some more, all told, in four tanks.

By this time, they were past Gauley Bridge, still following the river.

Someone who knows the territory has mapped this course for them. I wonder what they will do when we get to the Bluestone Dam, he thought.

Ahead was the bridge on Route 19 across the New River. Both planes passed over it in a flash.

"Five six one one bravo, West Virginia National Guard."

"Go ahead, National Guard."

"John, contact General Miller on 127.2. He is in his jeep on the way to the airport, we will monitor and you can talk to us if you want."

"Roger, Guard, five six one one bravo, over to 127.2."

"National Guard, National Guard, Aztec five six one one bravo."

"Five Six one one bravo, this is General Miller. We are convinced that the plane you are following is involved in a terrorist act. Can you continue to follow it while we get organized?"

"Affirmative, five six one one bravo. Be advised, I have two hours fuel at cruise power. Am now making one hundred sixty knots, just passing the Bluestone Dam. They have turned left to follow the Greenbrier River."

"Roger, we have called NORAD. They have scrambled fighters. Since the plane is civilian, we must coordinate our activities with the FBI. The Special Agent in Charge is Carter Cornick, based in Arlington. He is on a car phone on his way to the Manassas Airport to meet a helicopter. We will have you patched through to him shortly, stand by."

"Aztec Five six one one bravo, John, this is Carter Cornick, long time."

"Carter, I am just passing Camp Greenbrier, these guys are still making one hundred sixty knots. What do you want me to do?"

"Keep following, we expect them to turn north east any time. We could easily lose them in the mountains. Due to the limited range of attack helicopters, and their location, they won't be able to get into this for a while yet. Understand you have low fuel. Say duration now, please."

"Five six one one bravo has about one and one fourth hours fuel. These guys are flying past the

Greenbrier Valley airport now. Whoa, they just turned right through the notch at the old Greenbrier Airport. They seem to be following Interstate 64 now. Whoever planned this route for them really knew his stuff. I seriously doubt if they have showed up on anybody's radar yet. Now they are turning left up a valley, still holding low altitude."

Eight minutes later, he said: "They popped over the ridge south of the Hot Springs Airport and went back down into the next easterly valley."

"John, we have alerted everybody we can. We are convinced that this plane is headed for Washington. The parade is due to start in half an hour. Crowds are already bulging. The authorities know about your situation, but the public had not heard yet to our knowledge. The parade will take place as usual. The people in charge are afraid of a general panic if we call it off. How are you doing?"

"Still have visual contact. I am surprised they haven't spotted me. It has been daylight for some time now."

"What a deal. The helicopters will be later than earlier thought. You should be contacted by an F-15 any time. Call sign Ramparts. He will use this frequency. The plan is to shoot the 210 down over the Jefferson National Forest north east of you. If the device detonates, there will be casualties, but probably as few as anywhere. If they make it to the DC metro area, it will be real bad. What is your position now?"

"I am about twenty miles north east of Hot Springs Airport, down in a valley, beginning to worry a little about fuel. I am using up more than normal fuel with this low altitude. I can't lean the engines like at cruise altitude."

"Aztec five six one one bravo, this is Ramparts, do you read?"

"Read you loud and clear Ramparts, where are you?"

"I am about twenty five miles east of you, descending out of twenty, subsonic now. I am picking up your transponder, confirm you are still squawking 4444."

"That's affirmative, five six one one bravo."

"Keep on their tail until I get there, then I want you to drop back, in case the device detonates. I cannot use homing rockets for this because their heat signature is too small, but will have to use guns."

"Five six one one bravo, Roger. They are picking up a little speed now, maybe they have spotted me."

"This is really strange, five six one one bravo, I will be passing you with my gear down. I have you in sight now. Will overtake you on your right. If possible, wait till I tell you to back off. I still do not have them in sight."

"Roger, looking for you."

As he turned to the right to look up, the gray pointed shape of the F 15 came into sight, not a hundred yards away. Wow, what a sight. It overtook him in a few seconds.

"Drop back now five six one one bravo, I have them is sight."

"Roger, Ramparts."

As he watched, the F-15 closed up to within about two hundred yards of the 210. Then, all of a sudden, the

210 jinked to the right and disappeared. The F15 flew on up the valley, climbing.

"They must have spotted me, five six one one bravo, can you pick them up again?"

John turned to the right where the 210 had. They were nowhere in sight. He continued on. A minute passed.

"Ramparts, I have lost them. Where are you?"

"Back at ten, looking down for you. Turn on your strobes, please."

"Wilco. Still no joy."

"Giantkiller, this is Ramparts."

John could hear the F-15's half of the conversation while he transmitted on a VHF frequency and his frequency at the same time.

"Target lost temporarily. Orbiting above. Aztec still trying to reacquire." Then another pause.

"Roger."

"Five six one one bravo, Ramparts."

"Go ahead Ramparts."

"Any contact?"

"Negative. I am heading zero four zero. My DME reads 46 miles from Linden on radial 204."

"Aztec, Norad asks that you continue to try to reacquire the 210. I am to orbit above until you or I reacquire the 210 and try again. Helicopters are not doing as well as planned, still several minutes away."

"I see the 210. I see them."

"Roger, I will report. Try to close on them. I will report on the other frequency. Say airspeed."

"They must have fire walled it. Now one hundred seventy knots. I am gaining on them a little."

"Aztec, Norad wants the 210 downed before it gets to populated area. Whole DC area is ringed with helicopters and fighters now, but this guy could sneak through. Too many casualties to chance him getting to some populated area. If he realizes his mission is blown, he may divert to some population center to cause as much havoc as possible."

"Roger, Ramparts, and I am gaining on him. Do you see me yet?"

"Still negative. I have your transponder and will approach you from your six o'clock."

Now the Aztec was within two hundred yards of the 210. It would yaw once in a while to let one of them get a look at him.

Just then the F-15 descended in front of him and collided with the 210, John jerked the Aztec to the left and went to full power. He turned as best he could, but he watched out his right window as the 210's tail came off and it spun in. It hit the ground at cruise speed or more. There was a fireball, but only from gasoline. The F15 struggled to climb above the first ridge. He called.

"Aztec, I sure didn't mean to get that close. Couldn't decelerate as fast as I needed to. I have lost some of the leading edge on the left side. Windshield gone, leaking fuel big time. Gotta head for a field, any advice?"

"Not nearest but best would be Dulles. Can you make it?"

"Maybe, where are those helos?"

"Don't know, no contact. I am closing up with you. Can you get your gear up?"

"Negative, gear and flaps are inop. Thank goodness the gear is down, but it will severely restrict range. I don't feel so good, you take over the radio contact, let's go to Dulles."

"Roger, hang in there, Ramparts."

John quickly looked up the Washington Center frequency and called, "Washington Center, Aztec five six one one bravo with an emergency."

"Aztec five six one one bravo, Washington Center, continue squawk 4444, say nature of emergency."

"Aztec five six one one bravo is escorting a damaged F 15 fighter, after it collided with a Cessna, he has gear down and flaps down, but is leaking fuel. Windshield lost and pilot is injured. Request straight in to Dulles."

"Roger, five six one one bravo, stand by."

"Five six one one bravo, Washington Center has you in radar contact. Switch now to Dulles approach, on 128.95, they are advised of your emergency, good luck."

"Roger, thanks, Washington Center."

"Dulles Approach, Aztec five six one one bravo."

"Aztec five six one one bravo, this is Dulles Approach, describe situation."

"Dulles, Aztec five six one one bravo, level now at three thousand five hundred, escorting F-15 with injured pilot, airspeed one hundred sixty knots, he is leaking fuel and has leading edge damage, too."

"Roger, five six one one bravo, fly heading of zero three zero, descend to two thousand if you have to, you are cleared below, we show you thirty five DME from the field, report field in sight."

"Roger. Situation stable for now."

"Ramparts, how are you doing?"

"I am OK, Aztec, but I am not seeing too well, don't know what the problem is, I heard Dulles OK. It would help if you would fly in front and let me follow you. I can slow up a little more, since I am so light."

"Roger, I will increase to one hundred seventy knots. How about an echelon to my left?"

"OK Aztec, let's get on the ground soon, OK?"

"OK Ramparts. Only twenty to Dulles now."

"Dulles Approach, five six one one bravo has the field in sight."

"Roger, five six one one bravo, you will have expedited handling, contact tower now on 118.4, good luck."

"Thanks, Approach. See you."

"Dulles Tower, Aztec five six one one Bravo, with a friend."

"Five six one one bravo, Dulles Tower. Plan straight in runway one left, do you want the equipment?"

"Roger, Dulles Tower, Ramparts is injured and leaking fuel, may have some gear damage. Roll the equipment."

"Roger, five six one one Bravo, you are cleared to land."

"Dulles, five six one one bravo will need to land in formation with F-15."

"That is approved, five six one one bravo, good luck."

"Ramparts, how are you doing?"

"I'm OK, but losing some hydraulic pressure. I heard you say you wanted to land in formation. Should I close it up a bit?"

"Fifty feet or so is fine. I will stay slightly ahead to avoid tip vortices. Your gear is down and flaps down, OK. Do your pre-landing checklist, Ramparts."

"OK, Aztec, and thanks."

"What airspeed do you need to approach, Ramparts?"

"I need one forty knots."

"OK, I will wait till short final before I decelerate."

Ahead lay the numbers "1L" on the runway. The fuel was streaming out of the left wing of the F 15. John dreaded the possibility of a fire for Ramparts.

"All set, Ramparts?"

"Yeah, it looks good. A little mushy at this airspeed though."

"I am dropping back now Ramparts, I'll see you in the lounge."

"Roger, Aztec, thanks again."

John quickly pulled the throttles back, then tripped the gear lever. The nose wanted to come up as the gear came out. He put forward pressure on the yoke and moved the flap lever all the way down. The Aztec quickly decelerated and touched down to the left of the center line. Ahead the F-15 touched down. Everything seemed OK for a few moments, then the gear began to collapse. Ahead, he could see a foam truck, already foaming the runway. Another foam truck had a big area already done and the F-15's gear collapsed and it slid into the foam and disappeared for a moment in the spray. As he went by, almost to a stop now, he could see the firemen running to the F-15, to pull the pilot free. No fire.

He taxied to the ramp.

In about ten minutes, the firemen and the F15 pilot came into the lounge. He had a bandage on his forehead. They had him by the arms.

They shook hands as if they had known each other well. An FBO employee handed them each a Pepsi.

They collapsed into opposite chairs. Firemen, EMTs, military personnel came from everywhere.

On the television, they could see the President elect, riding in his limousine, waving to the crowd. I was a warm clear day for January. People were waving and shouting, it was a great day in Washington. He saw the President elect pick up something and hold it to his ear. Just then a white faced lady from the FBO office handed him a portable phone.

"Hello," was all he could muster.

"John, this is Fred. Thanks for what you did today for all of us. You and Major Denton will need to come have lunch with me next week. Get some rest. See you, and thanks again for all of us."

With that, the limousine stopped in front of the platform on the south Portico of the Capitol.

Suddenly, he was very tired.

10

PLAY COO

On Sunday mornings, we met at six AM. We called it the Dawn Patrol. We met and flew in the early hours, up the Ohio River, over the hills, down the valleys.

It must have been about forty degrees. There was still frost on the windshields of aircraft as I opened the door of Bates Aviation. The Quonset hut had made a nice office building at Tri State Airport. It was stark and cold, but it was home to us. As I got inside, I could see Debbie behind the counter. Her face was white as a sheet. She was on the phone. She looked up at me.

"What's wrong," I asked.

"Ralph has had a heart attack. He and Harold are at Play Coo. Oh, God!"

Play Coo was a play on words. Ralph and Harold had named their lodge in the wooded highlands of Mingo County after the mountaintop fortified area they had both tried to defend in Viet Nam. Plei Ku.

Kevin came in before another word was spoken, I told him what was happening. Debbie realized that she was holding the phone out away from her ear. She snapped it back to her ear.

"What do you want us to do?" She said into the phone.

"OK, hold on," she said and put the phone down on the desk.

"Harold wants Dad to come and get them quick," she said.

"Sounds like a good idea," I said.

"But Dad is in Cape Girardeau at the airplane auction. He took Mr. Bellinger last night. They are planning on buying him a plane today and flying back."

"Where are they?" Kevin asked.

"They are at Play Coo, the retreat they bought last fall."

"Where is that?" he asked.

"Southern Mingo County, just north of the Virginia border."

"Who can go, if your Dad is gone?" I asked.

She just looked at me.

"Me? Surely not. I don't even know where it is. Didn't you say that it had a short runway?"

"Yes, it's less than a thousand feet, but it has an uphill overrun to stop. Ralph and Harold take the 210 in there regularly. They flew down yesterday afternoon. Quick, they are giving Ralph mouth to mouth and oxygen from the plane." She was almost shouting.

I turned to speak to Kevin. He was gone. I bolted to the door. He was preflighting our 182, N5611 Bravo. I turned at the doorway.

"We are going, we will call you on unicom. The tower doesn't open until seven. When they do, telephone them, tell them where we are going. Do you have the lat long coordinates of Play Coo?"

"No, but I'll get them and call you. Go!"

I ran to the plane, Kevin had finished the preflight. I hopped into the left seat, shouting "Clear" before I hit the seat.

Kevin was an airline pilot for Northwest. He had just returned from a flight from Detroit to Beijing and return. He was still feeling like he was in a 747-400, not our little Skylane, so he was in the right seat.

The engine caught on the second blade. I released the brakes and the plane started to move as soon as the engine came to life. I let it idle at about eight hundred RPMs and pointed it toward Runway 12. As I put on my seat belt, he put my headset in place. Just before we taxied onto the runway, we checked the magnetos and broadcast, "Huntington Traffic, Skylane 5611 Bravo is taking Runway 12, southeast departure."

The engine had been awake for about three minutes total when I began to ease in the throttle. No hesitation. I slowly fed in until the knob stopped against the panel. The tach read 2600 RPM. Just as I noticed that, we eased off of the runway. I kept all of the lights on as we climbed into the morning twilight. Once we got to two thousand feet, I turned off the landing and taxi lights and kept the running lights on.

"I make the original course one six zero until we get better information. Best altitude would probably be five thousand five hundred with this temperature," Kevin said over the intercom and into my headset.

"How long do you think?" I asked.

"Twenty eight minutes about," he said.

"Charleston Approach, Skylane 5611 Bravo."

"Good morning Skylane 5611 Bravo, Charleston Approach."

"Charleston Approach, Skylane 5611 Bravo is off Huntington Tri State, squawking twelve, climbing to five thousand five hundred, with a request."

"Roger, 5611 Bravo, no radar contact yet, go ahead with your request."

"Charleston, 5611 Bravo has an emergency not involving the aircraft or occupants. We are trying to get to a private field in southern Mingo County to evacuate a friend who we believe has had a heart attack. We expect you will hear from Debbie Bates at Bates Aviation at Hotel Tango Sierra about the situation. It is a remote new strip near the Kentucky, Virginia, West Virginia border. We would appreciate your advice as to whether it would be closer to take the man to Charleston or Huntington."

"Stand by 5611 Bravo."

Three minutes, four minutes, five minutes.

"5611 Bravo, this is Charleston Approach. Distance from the field you describe would be closer to Huntington. Radar contact now, say intentions."

"Roger, Charleston Approach, the victim is fifty four years old, very overweight and has had alcohol problems. No knowledge of prior heart troubles. He is being given mouth to mouth and oxygen by non-professional personnel. Can you give us a vector based on coordinates of 37 40 North and eighty one thirty five West?"

"Stand by 5611 Bravo."

"5611 Bravo reached five thousand five hundred feet and leveled off. John left the throttle all the way in.

He gradually leaned the engine to best power, and followed in with trim to hold altitude."

"5611 Bravo, Charleston Approach."

"Go ahead Charleston."

"Fly heading of 171 magnetic. We estimate distance at four three nautical. Your ETA one five minutes. Can we be of further assistance?"

"Thank you Charleston Approach. We will stay with you."

Mingo County looks like an area that was once washed by strong waters and left high and dry. Its slopes are steep, its valleys narrow and torturous. Now with green trees over everything, it looked like a green blanket tossed into a wrinkled pile. All of the ridge tops were of consistent height, with a slight slope to the south.

Sunlight began to find the east-west lying valleys. Temperature at five thousand five hundred was five C.

"Debbie, this is John on 122.8 do you read?"

"Read you five by five," she said immediately. "Where are you?"

"We are about ten minutes from Play Coo. Tell me what you know about the runway there."

"It's about north-south. Land to the north. You will have about six hundred feet level, then the runway splits in a Y. The right fork goes up a graded slope about fifty feet in height to another flat area about three hundred feet long. The left fork goes back about three hundred feet to a high wall. Ralph and Harold said that if you were too fast on roll out, you could go up the hill to stop. The 210 should be tied down back to the left. Harold and Lew Buck are dragging Ralph down to the runway on a door they took off inside the cabin. Over."

"Thanks, Debbie. We will lose radio contact with you shortly as we descend for Play Coo. Charleston Approach says it is closer to Huntington. We will bring him there. Have an ambulance on stand by. We will land at Lawrence County."

"Will do on the ambulance. Call us when you are airborne. Thanks, guys."

The great expanse of Appalachian woods stretched before them, beside them and behind them. Kevin had a road map in addition to a Cincinnati Sectional.

"Best I can make out, we are about ten miles out, better get down to two thousand."

"Roger," said John as he pushed the yoke forward and pulled off a little throttle. The airspeed went up to one seventy and steadied.

"If we don't see it southbound, we'll overfly the Tug River and look for it from there."

"OK," said John.

"There is the river," said Kevin.

"The runway is over here," said Kevin. "We are just abeam."

"Great vector from Charleston, or what?" said John.

He pulled out more throttle and pulled on carburetor heat. The big Continental ran a little rougher as it swallowed the heated intake air. At two thousand feet, the 182 slowed predictably. John started a long arcing turn to base.

"What about wind, any problem?" He asked Kevin.

"Smoke from chimneys in the valleys indicate calm conditions. There will probably be some upslope breeze as the air warms, better factor in about seven knots of tail wind on final."

"I plan to bring it in on the prop, as slow as possible," said John.

"Good plan," said Kevin as he eyed the runway now at their two o'clock and four miles.

"Lights on, flaps coming down. Landing checklist."

Kevin read: "Carburetor heat."

John said: "On."

"Flaps set."

"Flaps now ten."

"Fuel on both tanks"

"Check."

"Mixture to full rich."

"Full rich, check."

"Seat belt tight."

"Seat belt tight."

"Starkeeper, stay with us."

John looked at Kevin.

"Starkeeper, stay with us," he repeated. Both men knew it wasn't just aerodynamics that kept planes aloft.

Now the airspeed was at seventy. John pulled on the last notch of flaps and added a little power to line up on final.

"Boy, it looks short," he said.

"Short and steep. Just keep the nose up, we'll be OK," said Kevin.

At about fifty feet above the runway threshold, the stall warning began to sound, growing in intensity until they arrived in the grass just beyond the edge.

Instantly John brought the flaps up and got on the brakes. At forty miles per hour, he put the flaps back down full for the extra braking. Occasionally one or the other wheel would lock in the wet grass and gravel. John would let up slightly, then try again. It seemed like an hour, but the landing roll was over in just seconds. They turned to the right and went up the slope where Harold and Lew Buck were waving them to come.

John turned the plane as tightly as possible next to the men. Kevin leaped out to help them get Ralph in the plane. As they started him into the back seat, John grabbed Ralph's wrist to help pull him in. He was at least two fifty and limp as a rag. His face was blue and his eyes were partly open. With the help of adrenaline, they got Ralph in.

Harold got in back with Ralph. Lew got in the front seat. Kevin stayed behind to bring the 210.

John added power to the idling engine and the 182 started toward the down slope. He held it back with the brakes until they were about half way down to the level part, then came in with power. He ran with no flaps until they were about one hundred feet from the far end drop off, then pulled on the flaps. The 182 responded with a graceful bound into the morning air. They hung on the flaps for some seconds as John leveled the plane and gained speed. There was no concern about clearing things on this end of the runway. The terrain dropped off steeply. They were already three hundred feet about the ground. As soon as he gained one hundred five miles per hour, he started a gentle turn to the left, climbing slowly.

Harold kept the oxygen going. It was an N bottle. John hoped there was enough to last another half hour.

Now they were at two thousand feet, climbing at one hundred forty miles per hour.

"Huntington Approach, Cessna 5611 Bravo." No answer.

"Heading is three four five," he said to Lew. Lew just nodded.

Lew was a helicopter pilot who flew the guys to the strip mines of Kentucky regularly.

John could see that Lew was deeply disturbed, maybe in shock over Ralph.

Now three thousand feet.

"Huntington Approach, Cessna 5611 Bravo."

"Five six one one Bravo, this is Huntington Approach, good morning."

"Huntington, 5611 Bravo is off private field Play Coo in southeast Mingo County, climbing through three thousand five hundred, squawking twelve, with a request."

"Roger, 5611 Bravo, go ahead with request, squawk 4435."

"5611 Bravo has four souls on board. One is a probable heart attack victim. We are taking him to Cabell-Huntington emergency room. We have ambulance on standby at Lawrence County Airport. You should have been contacted by Debbie Bates at Hotel Tango Sierra."

"Roger, 5611 Bravo, she advises Mrs. Hazelett is at the hospital. Ambulance is on standby at Lawrence County. Radar contact."

"Approach, ask West Virginia State Police if we can land on Sixteenth street extension and taxi to hospital."

Long silence, then, "Good idea, 5611 Bravo, stand by."

Two minutes, three.

"5611 Bravo, State Police advise they will clear and block off Sixteenth Street extension. Land toward the hospital. Taxi through the traffic light at Enslow

144

Boulevard into Big Bear parking lot. ER attendants standing by with gurney. Acknowledge."

"Thanks, Huntington Approach, good plan. How do we look on course?"

"Course good, maintain three four five. Report Huntington in sight."

"5611 Bravo has Huntington in sight. Looking for Sixteenth Street."

Now the narrow white snake of the access road appeared out of the green hillside. John jinked to the right to line up. He pulled off some throttle and began a shallow descent. As he began to run the landing checklist from memory, he realized that neither he, nor Harold nor Lew had spoken to each other the whole flight.

He snatched a look at Ralph, then at Harold. Ralph was light blue. Harold was white as a sheet.

Now carburetor heat. Now some flaps. Throttle back more, eighty miles per hour. They came down the valley south of the Interstate, then over it and touched down about half a mile beyond the interchange. They stabilized and taxied fast toward the flashing lights at the intersection of Enslow Boulevard. The officer waved them through with a pumping motion. Two hundred yards later, they turned right into the Big Bear Market's parking lot. He taxied up to the waiting attendants. All six of them pulled Ralph out. A doctor started an IV as they lifted him onto the gurney. He hung the plastic bag of fluids onto a steel rod sticking up from the gurney as they ran with Ralph toward the ER. John went over to the right main gear of the 182 and sat on the wheel. He was soaking wet.

11

NEWLON FIELD

Saturday was a precious time for us then. It was the day that you could go to the airport by the river and clean, shine, fix, service or just stand around and admire airplanes. John was just ready to close the access door on the bottom of the cowl of the experimental airplane that he had built the winter before. He had changed the oil and filter and was finishing up by putting a piece of safety wire from the plug on the bottom of the oil pan to a small loop of metal next to the plug. Working below the airplane in the grass, with the occasional drip of engine oil onto your clothes didn't allow one to keep his clothes clean for long. No matter, he was here, doing something he enjoyed with his fellows. What a peaceful way to pass a fine spring day. Robert Newlon Airport was on the east bank of the Ohio River, twenty three hundred feet of turf runway, a treasure of level land in an area of hills too steep and valleys too narrow to build a landing strip.

"Probably won't be too much flying out of here today," he thought, looking at the gray ceiling just a few hundred feet or so above him.

"It looks hard enough to knock on," he thought. From his tie down spot, he could hear and see the tug boat pass by with a barge tow of empties going upstream with a load of coal for the fiery furnaces of industry. The master waved as he passed. Even from under the airplane, John had a direct line of sight to the wheelhouse. He returned the wave.

Kevin, who had handed over the full cans of oil for John to pour into the funnel stuck into the filler and then bagged the empties, put his bag down with a clink into the barrel used for a trash bin. He turned and walked across the runway to the river bank tie down where the experimental sat securely tied to big steel spikes.

"I still think it was pretty slick to put that Bendix 2000 magneto on your engine. Most experimentals that use automobile engines have to put up with a single ignition source. Now you have the redundancy that certificated aircraft have."

John said, "I just thought one day about that big 10-720 engine in Bill's Comanche 400. It's the only eight cylinder aircraft engine I know of. It just occurred to me that we might use one of those mags to back up our regular ignition."

"Is it working out OK?" asked Kevin.

"Yes, but as you know, it has a set advance at twenty five degrees before top dead center. Without the vacuum or centrifugal advance of a car distributor, it would be severely limited above three thousand RPM. Luckily, with direct drive, we only use up to twenty eight hundred and that's only for full speed at altitude. Works pretty good. It's a factory rebuilt unit. So far so good."

"It's eight o'clock," said Kevin, "let's go over to the diner and get some breakfast."

"OK," said John, "but first let me secure this access door."

"John, I was hoping I would find you here." The voice belonged to Ron Carrier, John's next door neighbor and the Southern Methodist Minister at St. Paul's.

As John rolled over and squinted up at Ron, he could see by the set of his lower lip that Ron was under stress.

"What is it Ron?"

"We have a situation here. See that lady standing over there by my car? She is keeping her grandson from Lincoln County while his parents are in Cincinnati job hunting. She came into the food and clothing closet where I was volunteering in Hamlin just an hour ago."

"What kind of problem is there?" asked John.

"Dewey's mother and father are in Cincinnati job hunting. The family has been taking him to Duke University in North Carolina for treatment for a heart condition for a couple of years. He is on a waiting list for a heart transplant. Just an hour ago, they called from Duke. Seems that they have a heart that could be used for Dewey. His grandmother called me because she has no other help. I have called the airlines that fly out of Charleston and Huntington, but there is nothing on the airlines until about two this afternoon. That will be too late."

"Did you try the charter operations?" asked John.

"Yes, both airports are socked in, below minimums, they said and none of them would be able to go until the fog lifts."

"That would be right," said John. Both Yeager Field and Huntington are mountain top airports. They most likely would be socked in this morning."

"The boy doesn't have long. If he misses this heart, his condition will deteriorate to where they won't do the surgery. This may be his only chance. I thought you and your friends might know some way to help get him to Durham."

By this time, John, Kevin and Ron were standing in the still slightly dewy grass next to the plane. John and Kevin stood silent for a time.

Kevin, who flew a 747-400 for Northwest, turned and looked up the river. "Do you remember that old guy who told us that you could follow the rivers out of West Virginia into Virginia down between the mountains and never go over twenty five hundred feet above sea level?"

"Yes," said John. "We never checked it out, but he sure sounded like he knew what he was talking about."

"Let's get a chart and have a look," said Kevin.

They went to John's car and got a Sectional Chart out of the trunk. They spread it on the trunk as Ron came over to join them.

"Will that tell you if you can do it?" Ron asked.

"Yes," said Kevin.

"These charts have heights above sea level."

"Get your portable com," said John. Kevin went to his car and brought back a hand held radio.

"Let's listen to ATIS from Huntington. One two five point seven," said John.

Almost as soon as he had spoken the words, Kevin had tuned the radio and turned it up. "Huntington West Virginia Information India, this report compiled at thirteen ten zulu. Measured ceiling one hundred, visibility one quarter of a mile, fog and intermittent light rain, wind two eight zero at three, temperature twenty one, dew point twenty one, altimeter two niner niner six. On first call, say you have Information India."

"Well, that's below minimums all right. It's even illegal for a category one approach by an airliner."

"John, below the fog, here in the river valley, the visibility is a good five miles," said Kevin. "We could try to fly up the Ohio to Point Pleasant, then up the Kanawha past Charleston to Gauley Bridge, then follow the New River through the gorge. I have driven past Glen Lyn and through Narrows, Virginia many times. There is a break in the mountains there where the river passes through. I think the valley is wide enough all the way to make it. What do you think?"

"Remember those guys in the Grumman. They never found them, and that was just twenty miles from here."

"Yeah, the theory was that they hit a cable across the Ohio. Really too bad. But, you know, this isn't just about a pleasure flight. If we don't do something, we may be using up that boy's last chance," said Kevin.

"My biggest fear is the narrowness of the valleys, but if you will navigate, I will fly," said John.

The older woman had walked over to the men during the conversation and heard it all. She was sobbing softly. Her blue plaid dress looked like it had been washed and starched a thousand times. In the morning sun, it was clearly threadbare. She was wringing her hands like they had seen many women do in times of stress and grief.

"Can I help?" asked Ron.

"Help us pull the plane over to the gas pump."

The woman reached over to take John by the wrist. "God go with you mister, I don't know how I can ever repay you."

"That doesn't matter, ma'am. We'll do our best, now why don't you go get him ready?"

They pulled the plane over to the pumps and filled each tank to the top.

"Sixteen point three to fill them up. Now we have fifty six gallons, enough for four hours, plus reserve."

The little fellow was ten or so, but weak. Ron carried him to the wing.

"Will you go with us, ma'am?' asked Kevin."

"No, my mister is too sick to leave. Besides, I need to locate my daughter and tell her what's going on."

"Would it help if I went?" said Ron.

"If you want to chance it, you are welcome to come. Someone is going to have to watch out for Dewey during the flight. Kevin and I will have our hands full."

"I feel a need to go," said Ron. Kevin and John nodded. Nothing was said.

They put Dewey in the back seat and rolled up a blanket for a pillow. Jackets and other blankets quickly made a comfortable nest of that half of the back seat. Dewey was fully awake, but looked a little spacey. He smiled when John told him he was brave to fly in such weather with pilots he had never seen before.

After a little pat on his arm, his grandmother left him in Ron's care and climbed down off of the wing.

John waited three full seconds after calling a warning to stand clear before he engaged the starter. The prop started to swing slowly, smoothly gaining speed before the first sound of combustion disturbed the morning quiet. As it came to life, the gauges waved, raised, and moved to signify that there was oil pressure and revolutions were being made.

Kevin, who had rushed to his car trunk was still stowing charts and stuff in the floor in front of him. As they back taxied toward the north end of the runway, Kevin pulled the plug from the panel connecting John's two station intercom system to aircraft power. He plugged in another wire. John looked over for a second, curiously.

"Here, plug into this," said Kevin.

"I have a head set for Ron and Dewey. That way we can all hear and talk."

"Great first use for my new toy. Susan gave it to me for Christmas."

"Thank her for me," said Ron, over the newly powered up system. "I can hear you guys great."

At the end of the runway, John stopped and picked up the plastic laminated check list he had made.

"Let's see, oil pressure, OK, coolant temperature, OK, flaps set one notch, trim for takeoff, fuel set on left tank, controls free and correct, both ignition systems on. Let's check the ignition systems separately. Seems OK. Everybody set?"

"OK here," said Ron. Dewey managed an "uh-huh," and Kevin said. "Ready here."

John brought the RPMs up slowly, holding the brakes. When the power seemed to reach maximum, he quickly released the brakes and the plane surged ahead. At about six hundred feet down the runway there was a rise about six inches high. He usually was airborne before that, but this morning, the plane used the rise as a vault to spring into the air. Up between the trees on each side of the runway they came, now over the river and climbing toward that dark gray cloud deck. At about a hundred feet below the ceiling, John made a smooth right turn and brought them across the river and back toward the northeast over the far bank of the Ohio.

"This is about all the altitude we can hold now," said John.

"Seven hundred fifty MSL," said Kevin. "Looks like good clearance above the river and the visibility ahead is five or more."

"Dee always said when flying over the river to keep to the right side of middle just like a car on the road," said John.

"Use everything you know," said Kevin, "it's time."

"Let's keep a sharp eye for cables, even though they have to be below us at this altitude."

"I agree," said Kevin, "what concerns me is not what's here or in the next fifty miles, but what crosses the Kanawha river past Charleston. Sam Meads told me that their rule at the island airport they have at Belle is that if you are over the river and above four hundred feet above the river, you are safe to fly through the area."

In eighteen minutes they were nearing Point Pleasant.

"No other air traffic this morning," said Kevin.

"John, I have a question," said Ron.

"What does that plaque on the dash board mean, 'Experimental'?"

"It means that this plane was built by someone other than a certificated aircraft manufacturer, in this case, by me."

"Did you buy the design plans somewhere?"

"No, I designed it myself."

"I had no idea," said Ron. "Did you have difficulty getting a license for it?"

"No. The FAA inspectors from the district office were reasonable and friendly. They made some suggestions that I complied with. After some thought, I could see why they wanted the changes. It was sort of like they finished off a detail or two in the design."

"Does it have an aircraft engine."

"No, it's a Cadillac."

"I see," he said, but he had a quizzical look on his brow.

"We should see the Kanawha River in the next few minutes. Then the new bridge appeared. The old bridge had fallen into the Ohio, taking seventy lives in 1963. They all looked at the new bridge as they whisked overhead just four hundred feet above the river and three hundred feet above the bridge towers."

At the turn, they changed the radios to Charleston Approach frequency 124.1, just in case. The controller was talking to an airliner flying from Charlotte to Clarksburg.

"Technically, will we be in his airspace if we fly below field elevation up the river?" asked John.

"Gee, I never thought about that," said Kevin. "But as familiar as I am with the FAR's, I suggest that we call them as we go over the Bridge on 1-64 at Nitro."

"OK, can't hurt."

"Experimental 5611 Bravo, do you hear Charleston Approach?"

Kevin and John and Ron looked at each other. How?

"Charleston Approach, this is Experimental 5611 Bravo, go ahead."

"5611 Bravo, we received a call from the West Virginia Air National Guard. Seems one of their helicopters was at Cincinnati Lunken when the local police called to see if anyone was there going east toward West Virginia. The police brought the parents of your young passenger to Lunken. All the airports except Greater Cincinnati are socked in with fog and rain. Since they couldn't fly the parents to Charleston, they took them to Greater Cincinnati. They are now aboard USAir Flight 563 off Greater Cincinnati and estimating landing in Raleigh in one hour twenty minutes. The crew on Flight 563 relays a query."

"Go ahead, Charleston Approach," said John.

"Parents want to know if you want them to meet you at the hospital or the airport."

"Stand by," said John.

"What do you think I should tell him?" asked John.

Ron spoke first. "If they stay at the airport, there will probably be too many of us to all ride in one vehicle to the hospital."

"Good thought, said Kevin.

"May I?" he asked John.

"Sure," said John.

"Charleston Approach, 5611 Bravo."

"Go ahead, 5611 Bravo."

"Tell parents to go to the hospital. Ask them to have a vehicle standing by at Raleigh Durham."

"Roger, 5611 Bravo, by the way, did you file a flight plan?"

"Negative, 5611 Bravo would appreciate flight following, though."

155

"Roger, squawk 4456 and ident."

"5611 Bravo, radar contact three five miles north west of Charleston, your altitude readout indicates niner hundred fifty feet, confirm."

"That is correct, 5611 Bravo is level at niner hundred fifty feet."

"Roger, Charleston Airport is below minimums, say flight conditions."

"5611 Bravo has one hundred feet above us, estimated, visibility below clouds is at least five miles."

"Say type aircraft, airspeed, fuel and souls on board, please, 5611 Bravo."

"5611 Bravo is an experimental, one hundred fifty knots, four souls on board, four hours fuel."

"Roger 5611 Bravo, do you intend to land Raleigh Durham?"

"That's affirmative, 5611 Bravo."

By now they could see the giant smokestacks at the John Amos Power Plant. It was eerie to see the smokestacks disappear into the clouds above them.

"Fellows," Kevin spoke over the intercom, "Things may smell funny through this valley. There are a number of chemical plants which will pass below us. Don't be alarmed by the smells."

"OK," said Dewey whose eyes were locked on the smokestacks.

Past the bridge, past the island in South Charleston they call Magic Island, up the river valley through Charleston, many of its buildings sticking up into the clouds. Past the magnificent capitol with its gold capped dome.

"Now," said Kevin, "things may start to get a little more interesting."

"What do you mean," said Ron.

"The river narrows above Charleston. We will be flying through the New River Gorge well below the mountains."

"We may have to fly under the bridge on U.S. 19," said John.

"I expect so," said Kevin. "Plenty of clearance though, that bridge is almost a thousand feet above the river. Highest bridge east of the Mississippi."

As they passed the big ammonia tank at DuPont, Charleston Approach called again.

"Go ahead," said John.

"5611 Bravo, you are leaving our airspace, we really cannot suggest a center frequency for you because of your altitude, however, you might try us on this frequency if you need anything. You may be able to hear the Flight Service Station on the VOR frequency at Rainelle and broadcast on 122.1."

"Roger, Charleston, thanks," said Kevin.

"Oh, and 5611 Bravo, be advised, the media know about your flight. They have television cameras set up on the bridge at Route 19. People are gathering on the bridge. Use caution on over flying the bridge."

"Roger, Charleston, five six one one bravo does not plan to overfly the bridge."

"I see what you mean, five six one one bravo, but use caution anyway. Air traffic control authorizes you to use the call sign Lifeguard if you want. Have a safe flight you guys."

"Roger, thanks, 5611 Bravo," said Kevin.

"The weather is not getting any worse or better, I think," said Kevin.

"I agree," said John.

Just then they caught their first sight of the bridge. From four miles away, it looked like it had icing like a cake on it, but as they got closer, they could see that the entire bridge was covered with people. As they whisked under the bridge they could see the TV camera and people throwing flowers.

No one spoke for a while. After the bridge was out of sight, John tuned the navigation radio to one one six point six. The Morse Code signal of the Rainelle VOR came into each person's earphones. He turned the com radio to 122.1.

"Charleston Radio, Charleston Radio, Experimental five six one one bravo, listening on 116.6."

After about ten seconds, came, "Experimental 5611 Bravo, Charleston Radio, go ahead."

"Roger Charleston, 56 Bravo is about fifty east southeast of Charleston, going to Raleigh Durham. Could you give us the latest weather for a route of flight from Pulaski VOR to the southeast."

"Roger, 5611 Bravo, stand by."

"What did he mean by Lifeguard?" asked Ron.

"If you have organs for transplant or a transplant recipient on board, you can receive priority handling from air traffic control," said Kevin.

"Time to change fuel tanks," said John. "One hour off Newlon."

No change in the deep note of the engine after the change. John and Kevin watched the fuel pressure indicator for about five minutes. It never wavered.

Now they were passing over the Bluestone Dam. Just after the dam, they bore left over the New River.

"Kinda a narrow squeak between the dam and the ceiling," said John.

"About two hundred feet, I make it," said Kevin.

"Does it get narrower?" asked John.

"Somewhat, but the valley will open up before long."

In ten minutes, Kevin spotted the distinctive mountain shapes that told him they were approaching the Narrows.

"When we get to the Narrows, we will be in Virginia," said Kevin.

"What is your plan then?" asked John.

"I think we can clear the ridges ahead of us east of Radford. If we can, it is a straight shot to the piedmont of North Carolina."

But as they looked ahead the valley was sealed off in all directions. They had about eight miles to go to the ridge.

"What do you think?" asked John.

"If we cannot find a clear place, we can either land, turn around and go back, or climb through the overcast, file IFR and go to Raleigh that way."

"I'm not rated," said John.

"I am," said Kevin, "we'll file with me as PIC. Are you comfortable flying the aircraft on instruments?"

"Yes, but we are a bit light on navigation equipment," said John.

"If we have to, we can shoot the approach at Raleigh Durham using my handheld," said Kevin, "besides, they have PAR at Raleigh."

"What's PAR?" asked Ron.

"Precision Approach Radar," said Kevin.

"Basically the man in the tower guides you in direction and descent using radar at the runway. It is legal for him to talk us down to one hundred feet if necessary. Do you mind if we do this Padre?" asked Kevin.

"We are all in God's hands," said Ron. "Do what you think is best."

"Roanoke Approach, Experimental 5611 Bravo."

"5611 Bravo, this is Roanoke, go ahead."

"Roanoke, 5611 Bravo is approximately twenty miles north east of Pulaski VOR, VFR for Raleigh Durham, we would like clearance to climb to five thousand and proceed IFR to the South Boston VOR."

"Roger, 5611 Bravo, we were alerted to your flight by land line. Contact Roanoke Flight Service Station which is standing by to file and report back on this frequency."

"Roger, 5611 Bravo," said Kevin.

Shortly after they filed a flight plan and received their clearance, Roanoke Approach turned them over to Washington Center.

John trimmed the plane to climb at five hundred feet per minute and added power. Soon they punched into the clouds. The windshield streaked with raindrops. Gray ahead now.

"Three thousand now, what do we need to clear everything?" asked John. "Five Thousand will definitely do it, just hold a heading of one three zero. I will set the radios, one for Pulaski and one for South Boston."

"Washington Center, Experimental five six one one bravo, with you on 121.85."

"5611 Bravo, Washington Center, radar contact, squawk 1057 now, climb and maintain five thousand."

"Roger, Washington Center, 5611 Bravo climbing to five thousand."

"Your altitude readout indicates four thousand one hundred, 5611 Bravo, confirm."

"Roger, Center, 5611 Bravo is now at four thousand two hundred." Long gray minutes passed.

As the GPS indicated they were passing over South Boston, agreeing with the other navigation radio, they broke out into a clearing above the clouds. Now the vast expanse of cloud deck sprawled in front of them as far as they could see. Still holding one three zero, the little experimental hummed along, as if to say, "I knew I could do that."

"5611 Bravo, you are cleared now direct to Raleigh Durham. Use South Boston radial 172 until receiving Raleigh Durham. Report receiving."

"Roger, Center, 5611 Bravo."

Ten minutes later, still above a solid deck of clouds, John heard Center call. "5611 Bravo, contact Raleigh Approach now on 128.15, good day."

"Roger, Center, 5611 Bravo, thanks."

"Raleigh Approach, Experimental 5611 Bravo."

"5611 Bravo, Raleigh Approach. Continue and report receiving information Delta."

"Roger, 5611 Bravo."

Kevin tuned the radio to the Raleigh ATIS frequency.

"Raleigh Durham Information Delta. Ceiling one thousand overcast, visibility six, haze, wind two five five at five, temperature 28, dew point two zero, altimeter three zero zero eight, advise on first contact that you have information Delta."

"The field is below the clouds, Kevin, what do you want to do?"

"Ask them for a practice PAR approach. I will back up as good as I can with this handheld GPS."

"OK, you better take over the radios again."

"OK," said Kevin.

"Raleigh Approach, 5611 Bravo, requesting a practice PAR approach."

"Stand by, 5611 Bravo."

In a minute, Raleigh approach said, "5611 Bravo, cleared for practice PAR approach, expect runway five left, begin descent now to three thousand, report reaching."

John eased out a little on the throttle. In about a minute the little plane eased into the clouds below. Again the rain on the windshield.

"No turbulence, thank goodness," thought John.

"You are thirty miles from Raleigh, now 5611 Bravo, cleared on down to two thousand."

"Raleigh Approach, 5611 Bravo is out of three for two thousand."

"Roger, 5611 Bravo, turn right now to one six zero degrees and maintain two thousand."

"Roger, one six zero and two thousand for 5611 Bravo."

"5611 Bravo, you are ten miles from the runway, turn left to zero five zero, half standard rate turns. Transmit only if absolutely necessary and break off the approach if you do not hear a transmission from us at least every ten seconds."

"Roger Approach, 5611 Bravo."

"Kevin, let's switch tanks back to the left for the approach." The engine purred on in the gray.

"5611 Bravo, begin a five hundred feet per minute descent now, we show you seven miles from the runway threshold. Slightly right of course. Come left five degrees." The little airplane on the directional gyro wobbled around to zero four five degrees.

"Five miles from the threshold, now, on glide path and on course, continue 5611 Bravo."

As quickly as they had enveloped them, the clouds parted and there ahead of them was runway five at Raleigh.

"Approach, 5611 Bravo has field in sight, thank you."

"Roger, you are already cleared to land."

The wheels chirped down on runway five. They quickly called ground control.

"Roger, 5611 Bravo. Taxi to the ramp via taxiway Kilo, left at the second intersection. The ambulance is waiting in front of Stevens Aviation."

"Roger, Ground, thanks."

As they taxied up, John cut the engine and opened the door. The ambulance attendants were on the wing in seconds. In less than two minutes it was over, the ambulance left 5611 Bravo at the ramp. Ground personnel gently eased it into a tie down and there it waited to take its masters home.

"Thanks mister," he said softly, then the orderly wheeled him off down the hall, his mother and father at his side. About sixty feet away, he leaned around the back of the wheelchair and smiled at them. It was good.

12

HOT SPRINGS

Still a little stiff from those long hours over the water, Kevin hauled himself out of his old BMW and ambled across the ramp toward the office. The airport on this Thursday afternoon was hot and quiet. There was a buzz coming from the depths of the hangar where someone was operating an air driven tool. The hangar would be the coolest place to be today, unless it was the air conditioned office. He had agreed to fly with Bill to take a passenger charter to Boston in Bill's Conquest because Bill needed a good "right seat" for the trip and because he wanted to get some time in the turboprop twin for his logbook. Since the Supreme Court had recently upheld the Federal Aviation Administration's age sixty retirement policy for airline pilots, he knew that it wouldn't be too long before he would be put out to pasture, and he could envision flying a turboprop or jet twin for a corporate client as a good follow on to his present job as Captain of a 747-400 flying from Detroit to Hong Kong.

The plane was sitting on the tarmac in front of the office and Bill was getting ice for the cooler when he first saw Kevin.

"Hey, how's it goin'?" Bill asked.

"Fine," said Kevin. "Thanks for the invitation."

"With the light load, and the winds aloft forecast, I make the odds eighty-twenty that we can make Boston direct. We'll make our decision over Harrisburg and land for fuel at Farmingdale if necessary. That sound OK to you?"

"Sure, will we be there long?"

"Naw, quick turn around. Should be home by ten tonight."

"That'll work. What do you want me to do?"

"File our flight plan and get the charts ready. I'll do the walk around with you in about fifteen minutes. We'll have only one passenger, someone from Vanderbilt. He's taking something to Boston and will return with us."

Kevin knew as he sat in the hot right seat that soon after they took off, the need would be to get enough heat, not cooling, so he patiently folded the High and Low Altitude Navigation Charts that they would need, and got out the Approach plates for Boston Logan. Bill did say the big airport, didn't he?

Once Bill had iced the cooler, he and Kevin did their walk around inspection. Learning as he went, Kevin tried to absorb everything Bill pointed out about the twin.

"This one has the Garrett engines," Bill said. "Great high altitude performance, a little noisy on the ground, though. These engines have three hundred hours on them since a hot section check. How did you like the GPS?"

"I love GPS," said Kevin. "We use it on the 747. It really tells you what you need to know."

A dark gray Chevy suburban pulled up in front of the office. Four men got out, two in uniforms and with weapons, the other two in shirts and ties. One had a large suitcase. As they approached the plane, one of the two in civvies asked, "Are you Bill Gordon?"

"That's me," said Bill, "Are you Mr. Armentrout?

"Right. Is it OK if Mr. Baldwin goes along? I'd really appreciate it."

"No problem on weight and balance, but it just might make the difference as to whether we have to stop for fuel, is that OK with you?" asked Bill.

One of the uniformed men said, "Mr. Armentrout, we'll stay until you are in the plane and have taken off. We'll go after you depart. Have someone please call our office if you have to return for any reason and we'll have someone get back out here."

"OK," said Mr. Armentrout.

Both passengers took the rear seats and Bill and Kevin went forward after securing the air stair door.

When the first engine started, Bill turned the fan up to maximum to clear the hot air from the cabin. Kevin called for the clearance.

"Roger, Twin Cessna 52466, cleared to Bravo Oscar Sierra as filed, except Elkins VOR is out of service, cleared from Hotel Victor Quebec to Echo Sierra Lima, then as filed, high altitude refueling practice is scheduled to take place east of Charleston along J45 after 2100 hours, center will keep you advised, expect twenty four thousand ten minutes after departure, departure on 125.65, squawk 4011, altimeter is 30.12, wind is 250 at eight, freezing level is fourteen thousand, contact ground on point niner when ready to taxi."

Kevin read back the clearance and called ground control. Taxi was handled by Bill and Kevin read him the before takeoff checklist at the run-up area. With takeoff clearance from the tower, they started to roll. The Cessna accelerated much quicker than the big 747 that Kevin was accustomed to. With a rush, they were aloft. Then Bill flicked the gear switch to the up position and the plane accelerated again with the additional drag of the landing gear disappearing into the wells.

"Approach, Twin Cessna 45266 is with you, climbing on runway heading through two thousand."

"Roger, Twin Cessna 45266, turn left to two seven zero and climb and maintain six thousand."

"Left to two seven zero, and up to six thousand, 45266," Kevin said.

As they were passing through five thousand five hundred, Approach called again. "Twin Cessna 52466, turn left to zero eight five, climb and maintain eighteen thousand, report reaching."

"Roger, approach, 52466 is turning left to zero eight five and out of six now for eighteen."

As they climbed through ten thousand, Mr. Baldwin came forward and squatted slightly behind them. Bill didn't like having passengers moving about and he didn't like this man coming forward to the cockpit. Just as he was about to say something to Mr. Baldwin, Mr. Baldwin spoke, "I hate to disturb you gentlemen, but there has been a change in plans.

"What do you mean?" asked Bill, clearly startled.

"In case you didn't know it, that case that Professor Armentrout is holding contains the LaRue Diamond collection which has been on display at Vanderbilt. It will not be proceeding to Boston as planned."

He had been holding his right hand just out of their sight until that moment. As he showed them his automatic, he said. "We are holding Professor Armentrout's wife and daughter. He has been most cooperative. If anything goes wrong, my associates will have to think of some imaginative way for them to disappear. Call and cancel your flight plan."

Almost in disbelief, Bill's mouth slacked open. Kevin began, "Center, Twin Cessna 52466 is canceling its IFR flight plan at this time."

"Any problems, 52466?" said the Center Controller.

"No," said Kevin, "just a change in destination, thank you and good day."

"Now, turn off the communications radio and the transponder and pull their circuit breakers. If you attempt to turn them back on, it will be most unpleasant. I am familiar with aircraft and I will be sitting in the middle seat back there where I can see the panel. Do it now, captain," said Baldwin.

Bill's face reflected anger and fear at the same time as he reached over and turned off the communications radios and the transponder. The circuit breakers were on Kevin's side of the panel, so as Bill directed, he pulled them, too. The lights blinked out on the affected radios, leaving a black hole in the middle of the panel.

"What do you want us to do?" asked Bill.

"Plan on landing at Hot Springs, Virginia, taxi up to the aircraft holding at the south end of the runway.

When I get on the plane with the diamonds, we will release the wife and daughter from the plane. No funny business, gentlemen. Use your heads."

With the com radios out, Bill and Kevin still had their intercom function working. With all the noise of the cabin, Baldwin, if that was his name, couldn't hear what they would say to each other, but what use is talk? They had their instructions. This was a dangerous errand now. Professor Armentrout looked genuinely miserable in the back seat. Now that Baldwin had told us what was happening, Armentrout was free to express some of the misery he had been expertly hiding since earlier that day.

Kevin dug out his low altitude chart for the sector. He had landed at Hot Springs three times before and knew the area very well. Years ago Kevin and Peggy had spent a few get away weekends near there and enjoyed the high mountain weather in the heat of summer.

"How long, at this speed, will it take us to reach Hot Springs?"

After a quick look at the chart and the DME, Kevin said, "About an hour."

"Got any ideas?" Bill asked calmly.

"Just one. Do you think he can see me as well as he can see you and the panel?" Kevin asked.

""No, that curtain is pulled back toward your side. It partially blocks his view, especially to your right."

"Let's try to buy some time, set up the course to zigzag from Beckley to Pulaski, that should add twenty minutes. If you will look busy with the panel resetting the navigation radios for a few minutes, I have an idea," said Kevin.

Without moving the rest of his body, Kevin slowly fished into his "brain bag" with his right hand. He was grateful to feel the portable transceiver. With only a small output, it was most doubtful that anybody would hear his transmission, but with their altitude and holding it next to the window, it might just reach out enough. He dared not call a mayday, that might provoke some kind of aerial pursuit, which would doom the hostages. What to do? What frequency to call on? Who to call? What to say? His mind raced.

"Where are we, he asked himself. Twenty minutes out of Nashville, level at Flight Level 180, on a heading of zero eight five. That should put us near Jacksboro. That's sixty miles northwest of Knoxville. Maybe, just maybe, it will reach. It's fully charged up. It's our only chance, I guess. Something needs to be done soon, if we want to try anything. He took a long slow breath, tried his best to compose himself, and thought about the alternatives. What to do? Who could possibly help? If these guys see a uniform, they will use the hostages to escape. If it gets rough, they will kill the hostages. The Professor looks sick with worry. I would be too."

"Please, Starkeeper, these people need my help. Guide my thoughts, stay with us this dark night. Bring these helpless people through, if it is your will, Amen."

The hangar door was open. John and R.D. were working in the early evening on John's experimental airplane, now almost ready to be signed off by the FAA. They had flown off the required twenty five hours in the local area and called the District Office of the FAA to have an inspector come down and hopefully sign off one of the latest additions to the civil fleet. They were both under the right wing on creepers adjusting the landing gear door. In flight, R.D. had spotted it hanging about a half inch down with the gear up. Just a detail, but attention to detail was one of the things that gave an aircraftsman the satisfaction of a nicely finished homebuilt.

The airband scanner on the shelf crackled as it changed frequencies. Tower, approach to the east, approach to the west, center, emergency, and unicom for the small airpark south of the big airport had been set to be scanned in order. With that new digital feature, you could change frequencies easily. Much better than those old scanners that used crystals.

"I need a seven sixteenths open end for that jam nut," said John.

"It's on the floor, just behind you," said R.D.

Just as he picked it up, the scanner switched from Approach to the next channel.

"R.D., R.D. I sure hope you have your scanner on. This is Prop Wash. We have an emergency and I cannot call ATC."

John and R.D. looked at each other without speaking.

They rolled their creepers as quietly as possible out from under the wing, climbed off and quickly walked over to the scanner on the bench.

"R.D., I sure hope you are at the airport with your scanner on. This may be my only chance to broadcast. I am using my handheld, so this may be faint. I am right seat in a Cessna Conquest, call sign November 52466, on heading of zero eight five off of Nashville, level at Flight Level One Eight Zero. Our cargo of diamonds is being hijacked by a group of people. One is on board, holding a gun on us. There is a Vanderbilt Professor named Armentrout on board. He was the custodian of the diamonds that were on display at the museum. We were returning them to Boston. This guy who calls himself Baldwin told us to turn off our com radios and transponder and to cancel our IFR flight plan. We have been told to land at Hot Springs, Virginia, and taxi to the south end of the runway where a plane is waiting. Once Baldwin gets on board, he says, they will free Mrs. Armentrout and a daughter, age unknown. If any cops or the like appear at Hot Springs, I think they will use us all as hostages to get out. I have no doubt that they will hesitate at nothing to get the diamonds. I am not going to call the authorities. I am transmitting this on our favorite air-to-air frequency for privacy and because I know it is programmed into your scanner. I hope you are there. You are our only hope. We estimate Hot Springs in one hour. We will try to zigzag from Beckley to Pulaski to buy a little time, but that may be detected and scuttled. We will try to throttle back to lengthen the time, but he may see that too and correct us. Baldwin is Caucasian, male, five feet ten, dark hair, mustache, looks about forty, weighs about one eighty, speech is with mild European accent, but I did not hear enough to say more about that. Blue eyes, no tattoos or visible scars. Weapon is a Beretta nine millimeter. Professor Armentrout is about forty five, looks fit, but he is distressed right now. We have had no opportunity to talk with him since this erupted. Baldwin is sitting in the middle right seat behind me. He cannot see this transmitter, but I am going to put it back in the brain bag and take no chances. Good Lord, I hope you are listening. Use caution if you try anything. The other members of the group are probably heavily armed. I suspect that they have a long distance airplane waiting and will use terrain to block their departure direction and will pop up far away, but that is just a guess. We have no com radios or transponder, but you could try to reach us on the VOR frequency of Beckley or Pulaski or the Hotel Sierra non directional beacon at Hot Springs if it is still operational. We have earphones and intercom, so as of now he cannot hear anything we say to each other or what we receive, but that may change, so be careful if you transmit anything to us. This is your old buddy Prop Wash, leaving the air."

Neither man spoke for several seconds, each absorbing what they had been told and putting the beginnings of a plan together. What to do? How to do it? Mercy!

Almost unnoticed by John and R. D., Glenn Barth, a local pilot and oral surgeon, walked into the hangar and up to where they were standing while Prop Wash's broadcast came through. The three men looked at each other, each one's mind whirling with alternatives and questions.

R.D. spoke first. "Sure wish we had our Conquest here. We need speed. No way, though, it's in Dayton."

"Even if we could get there in time, what could we do?" asked John.

"If you go, I want in," said Glenn. Glenn had been Army Special Forces before and after Dental school, a good man to have on your team in such circumstances.

John said, "As I see it, we need to go immediately and compose a plan in the air on the way. I have a .45 in the car."

R.D said, "Your Cherokee certainly isn't fast enough to get us there in time. Is there anyone else here with a fast plane?"

Glenn said he would take a quick look and sprinted from the hangar.

"Preflight your plane," R.D. said to John. Without questioning, John ran to do so. Typically, it was ready to go when backed into the T-hangar. Fuel was topped up. He needed only to check the oil level, top that off and preflight, which he immediately did.

Glenn came back in. "There is no one. No fast plane, nothing. All the jets are out. Where does that leave us?"

"As I see it, we have to take the Experimental, and soon," said R.D. "Let's get airborne."

The only thing Glenn retrieved on his running trip across the tarmac was a silver cylinder and a pair of camo coveralls. R.D. had on a dark blue jacket and jeans. John had his leather flight jacket over a dark green golf shirt and jeans. R.D. smirked to himself as he swung into the cabin that the only weapon he had was a pocket knife.

"Knoxville Clearance, Experimental 5611 Bravo, with information India, ready to taxi at the T-hangers," spoke John into the headset.

"Roger, 5611 Bravo, plan to taxi to Runway two three left, say destination," said Clearance.

"Just up to Downtown airport for some night landing practice, 5611 Bravo."

"Roger 5611 Bravo, contact Ground on point eight."

"Roger, Clearance," John said as the experimental rolled toward the taxiway.

"Ground 5611 Bravo, to Downtown, with India."

"Roger 5611 Bravo, taxi to 23 left."

"5611 Bravo, Roger, 23 left."

"Tower, Experimental 5611 Bravo is ready to go on two three left."

John had checked the mags on the roll and moved the controls to their limits and otherwise prepared quickly for flight, his first night flight in his newly signed off experimental homebuilt airplane. There were three seats: two in front, side by side, one behind those, facing sideways. Glenn was already in the plane and strapped in by the time John and R.D. got in.

"Experimental 5611 Bravo, cleared for takeoff, Runway 23 fly runway heading."

"Roger, 5611 Bravo is rolling and would like an early left turnout."

The power came up with a surge and the plane lunged down the runway. In just a little longer than it takes to say it, the plane lifted off. As soon as he reached Vy, John reached up and retracted the landing gear.

"Five six one one Bravo, left turn out at this time, contact approach on 125.9, have a nice flight."

"Roger, Tower, 5611 Bravo, left turn now and over to approach, good evening."

"What is your plan, R.D.?" asked John.

"When approach hands us over to Downtown, we will tell Downtown we are going to the north practice area, then we'll scoot for Virginia."

"What is your best altitude for speed?" R.D. asked.

"We'll find out tonight, but my guess is about seventy five hundred."

"What is your best speed to date?"

"One hundred eighty knots."

"Will that get us there in time?" asked Glenn.

"My guess is that it won't," said John, "but we'll try our best. We have four hours fuel on board at full power. I don't plan to pull the throttle back any time after we leave the pattern at Downtown."

"Five six one one Bravo, contact tower at Downtown, good evening."

"Thanks Approach, 5611 Bravo."

"Downtown Tower, 5611 Bravo, request."

"Go ahead 5611 Bravo, this is Downtown Tower."

"5611 Bravo would like to go to the north practice area before returning to land."

"That's approved 5611 Bravo, report inbound."

"Great," said John to R.D. and Glenn. "Now let's see what this baby will do."

"What do you estimate your actual horsepower?" asked R. D.

"We have four hundred fifty five cubic inches with a compression ratio of only seven point five. At twenty seven hundred RPMs, I estimate we have two hundred sixty horsepower. We have about the same flat plate drag signature as a Mooney 252, and we are right at max gross weight. What do you make our best course to Hot Springs?"

"Been figuring, glad we brought this portable GPS. It says HSP direct is zero eight two, one hundred seventy four nautical miles. If we beat one hundred seventy four knots, we can make it in less than an hour. Do either of you think we should alert ATC or the FBI?"

Long silence.

Glenn spoke first, "You guys should decide about ATC. As for me, let's think a few minutes before we decide on the FBI."

"I'm against calling ATC. They don't have any resources to help and they will surely call in the feds if we tell them what is really happening. The way I see it, we either succeed or fail by ourselves. If we call in help, the hostages may be harmed. I'd rather fail than get someone hurt. Besides, they may turn loose of the hostages after they get the diamonds," said John.

"Remember our friend Carter Cornick is with the FBI in Richmond. I would trust him to handle the situation right," said R.D.

Glenn relented, "We are clearly outgunned now, maybe your friend in the FBI could help, but how do we get in touch with him?"

"Do you want me to call," asked John, looking at both of them. They both nodded.

John turned a dial on his com radio. "Roanoke Radio, Roanoke Radio, Experimental 5611 Bravo, on one twenty six point niner."

After about ten seconds came, "Experimental 5611 Bravo, this is Roanoke Radio, go ahead."

"Roanoke Radio, Experimental 5611 Bravo has an unusual request. We have an emergency other than with the aircraft. We want you to patch us through to the FBI number in Richmond, Virginia, please. Can you do that, over."

"The state police have a phone patch, I can try that, stand by 5611 Bravo."

"'I guess we have to take the chance," said John. No one disagreed.

"5611 Bravo, I have Sergeant Patterson on the line, go ahead."

"Sergeant Patterson, this is John Hache, I am a private pilot in an experimental single engine airplane heading north east up the valley of Virginia. With me are my brother R.D. Hache, an airline transport pilot, and Glenn Barth, a private pilot, and former Special Forces Major. A friend of ours is flying an airplane that has been hijacked out of Nashville, and we need to talk to Carter Cornick at the FBI office in Richmond. Can you patch us through?"

"I'll try, stand by." Long seconds. One minute, two minutes, three minutes.

"5611 Bravo, FBI duty officer Special Agent Cornick is at church tonight. I am trying to reach him there, stand by." More long seconds.

"5611 Bravo, we have Mr. Cornick on the line, I will monitor if you don't mind."

"Thank you sergeant, we need all the help we can muster."

"This is Carter Cornick, John, long time no see. What's up?"

John brought Carter up to date.

"Wow, you really do have a tiger by the tail."

"Sergeant Patterson, how quickly could you have a team up there?"

"Our closest man Nolan, is at a PTA meeting in Covington. He is at least a half hour from the airport. He has a beeper and I can reach him. Do you want me to?"

"Yes, said Carter, go ahead and alert him. Minutes count."

"John and RD, what is your plan?"

"Try to beat our buddy to Hot Springs, and stand by to seize any opportunity to free the hostages. We have only one firearm with us, a .45 auto. I believe if we can beat the Conquest there, we might be able to do something, but we may have to see what we have there before we decide. It looks like it will be pretty spontaneous."

"Roanoke Radio, thanks for your help, will it be any problem to keep this line open for a while. I am on a cell phone in the assistant pastor's office, standing by."

"No problem, sir, we'll keep the line open."

"Gentlemen, I have reached Master Trooper Nolan, he is proceeding as fast as possible to the airport. He is driving an unmarked black Ford without lights and siren at this time. He estimates the field in thirty five minutes. He has a handgun and an M-16 in the trunk. I have him in radio contact and will maintain contact with him. He will approach quietly. He knows you are armed."

"Here's a thought," said John. "Hot Springs has only one paved runway, about fifty six hundred feet long. The hoods are in a plane at the south end of the runway. What if we land on the old grass cross runway without lights and try to sneak up on them? There is no way we can land conventionally without alerting them. I don't think they can see the threshold of the old grass runway from where they are parked. There is a little ridge on the southeast comer of the airport that obstructs that view. If we can come in without power and without lights and touch down close to the threshold, they might not see us and they almost surely will not hear us if they are all in their plane."

"The only other asset that I can muster at this time is possibly the state police helicopter, but it is in

Blacksburg, and the pilot is off duty. I don't know if I can reach him in time. He may have not taken his beeper tonight," said Sergeant Patterson.

"About the only thing I can contribute from here is advice and follow-up in a little while. Do we know what type aircraft they have waiting at Hot Springs?" asked Carter.

"No, we don't," said R.D., "but we assume it is long range and six or more seats, probably a turboprop or a small jet. My theory is that they will depart to the north to avoid Roanoke radar, then turn around and go down the valley under radar coverage until they can pop up and file a flight plan under some bogus registration number and scram to far away places. On the other hand, they really don't need to go far on the first leg, no one will know what means they will use to travel after the airplane at Hot Springs. They could ditch it quickly and change to another plane or something else. Then they are really going to be hard to find."

"We can probably be on their tail pretty quick, even if you guys can't stop them," said Carter.

"We only need a few extra minutes and we can have a Coast Guard HS-125 in position. He was offshore looking at a suspicious boat until I called him. He is now just crossing the coast, feet dry they call it, and is making four hundred knots toward Hot Springs. He estimates forty minutes, though."

"What is your ETA Hot Springs, now, John?"

"Twenty minutes," said R.D.

"Have you heard anything from your friend since the first radio call, R.D.?"

"No, but we have the second com radio set to the frequency he transmitted on, just in case." said R.D.

"That Victor airway passes almost over the airport on the south side. Why don't we fly over just like regular traffic so we can get a look, then proceed a few miles east, turn off the lights, and make a quiet approach to the grass runway?" asked John.

"Sounds like the best bet. Are there any other landing strips close?" asked R.D.

"There is a grass strip built by the Corps of Engineers in 1938 about six miles north east. Thirty eight hundred feet long, eighteen hundred MSL."

"Gee, how did you know that?" asked R.D.

"The morning Jay was borne, I 'flew' through that valley in my Plymouth Barracuda on the way to Charleston. When I saw the windsock, I promised myself that if I ever got to be a pilot, I would return someday and land there. We could land there, but we would not make it to Hot Springs Airport in time."

"Pays to know the territory, doesn't it?" said Glenn.

"Your plan sounds fine to me," said Carter, "Just be careful. Remember the important thing is that the hostages are much more important than the planes or the diamonds."

"Hot Springs Airport is about ten miles at eleven thirty," said R.D. All of them strained to the left windows to see what they could as they whisked over the ridge top airport. There was a plane at the south end of the runway.

"A Cheyenne," said R.D. They flew on at seventy five hundred feet. Two minutes later, John turned off the running lights, turned left and said, "Here we go. Once we get on the ground, Glenn, you be in charge?"

"OK," said R.D. and so did Glenn. "Do you want my .45?" asked John. "No, you keep it," said Glenn, "I have some ideas. Do you R.D.?"

"Yes, but we still don't know if Kevin will have had any success with Mr. Baldwin before they get here. We need to neutralize the Cheyenne and be waiting for them when they arrive. I suggest that we smear our faces with mud as we run toward the Cheyenne. If we can get close, we might be able to disable the plane from outside, but that will only bring someone boiling out. That is where you are going to have to suggest something Glenn," said R.D.

"Airspeed is at gear operating speed, gear coming down, flaps pumping down now, too. I hope there are no deer or big rocks in the runway. Glad I painted this plane dark grey. Sure hope they aren't outside. They could hear us land."

"If they do, they'll probably scoot," said Glenn. "Go ahead with the plan, I believe this is our best shot."

At seventy knots, the experimental eased over the threshold, nosed up a little and touched down in the deep grass. No one had mowed since they stopped using that runway years ago. There were thick weeds in patches, up to three and four feet deep, but most was timothy hay and gentle to pass through. The plane came to a quick stop just five hundred feet from where it touched down. They very quietly got out. And immediately began loping toward the other end of the runway. A careful run, not full speed, but not slow either. The Cheyenne was dark. The air stair door was closed. No sign of occupants. They sneaked up to the right of the plane keeping bushes between them and the plane. At about forty feet, they stopped and lay down with their heads close to each other.

"I think I should let the air out of the right main tires," said R.D. "That will keep them here until someone re-inflates them. When they come out, we can grab one or two, what do you think?"

"Good idea," said Glenn. "John, you position yourself where you can get a clear shot at the air stair door. You choose the range, but not too far, be sure of yourself. Don't shoot unless you have to, but don't hesitate if you need to shoot."

"OK," gulped John and began sneaking around to the tail end of the plane.

"This cylinder has a new anesthetic gas that I have been asked to try by a pharmacy manufacturer, is there an inlet for cabin air that I could squirt this into, maybe to knock them out?" asked Glenn.

"Sure, on the nose, right side about three feet back is a streamlined inlet. But won't the gas flow make too much noise?" asked R.D.

"I think I can keep it quiet enough, do you think it is worth a try?" asked Glenn.

R.D. nodded. So they crawled as carefully as they could toward the Cheyenne. Still no sign of the approaching Conquest. R.D. stripped off his shirt and held it over the valve as he let some nitrogen out of the outboard main gear tire.

Haven't done a trick like this since Halloween when we were kids, he thought. Soon, the tire sagged. He repeated on the inboard. Glenn had reached the cabin air inlet and was training a stream of gas into it. Luckily, the pilots had a blower going to keep cool and the noise masked the noise of the gas flow and helped draw the gas into the cabin. R.D. crawled out under the wing and stood up outboard of the right engine. Through the windows, he could see a woman and child huddled in the rear seats. A man and woman were in the center seats. Two pilots in place up front. No sound except the whine of a blower. He took his shirt and stuffed it into the air intake.

"There, that ought to prevent this engine from starting, but they will probably start the left one first, like usual," he thought. So he ducked under the wing and crawled under the plane to the outboard of the left engine. Since he had used his shirt on the right engine, he peeled out the liner of his jacket and reached to stuff it in the intake. Just as he got his hand in the intake, the left engine started to turn.

"They are getting ready! Then the air stair door opened. Strange."

The man came down the stairs. "Got to get some air," he said. Just as he got to the bottom step, Glenn tackled him, pinning his gun under him. It went off under him, but the bullet hit only dirt. The muzzle flash burned his belly though and he cried out. Just as the woman stuck her head out the air stair door to yell, "Carlo, what the hell?" R.D. reached up and grabbed her by the hair and flung her out onto the ground. Her pistol fell aside. She lay still.

"Mrs. Armentrout, come out, your husband sent us," said John.

They immediately bolted out the door. Strangely, the pilots didn't move. Not so strange, really. Once Mrs.

Armentrout and her daughter were safely with R.D. heading for a hiding place off the edge of the runway, John eased his .45 and then himself into the cabin of the Cheyenne. The pilots were sound asleep. One had his hand near the start switch for engine number one. They stirred as he waited a minute.

"What hit us Ernie?" said one.

"Dunno, hey, who are you?"

"Never mind. You guys just sit tight for now, no funny business," said John, making sure that they could see his weapon.

Glenn had confiscated the man's weapon, gathered him up, made him carry the woman over to the edge of the runway where R.D. had the Armentrout women hidden. Above he could hear the whine of the Conquest approaching, turning a left downwind for Runway 24. Landing without lights, it ghosted down final and made a good quiet landing and rolled, slowing as it came to the south end of the runway. As it got close, it stopped about fifty feet away beside the Cheyenne, so that its air stair door was toward the air stair door of the Conquest. No sooner had it stopped than the air stair door opened. Baldwin started down the stairs unsteadily. Just as he got about halfway down, Armentrout tackled him from behind. Glenn reached them before Baldwin could recover and get his gun out from under him. The smell of vomit was strong.

"Friends, Professor Armentrout," said Glenn as he helped wrestle Baldwin away from Armentrout. Quickly out of the Conquest were Kevin and Bill, but by then Baldwin was at gunpoint.

"Since you are holding a gun on Baldwin," can we assume you are police or something?" asked Kevin.

"Not police, but friends," said Glenn. "Your friend R.D. has Mrs. Armentrout and daughter safe over there by the edge of the runway." Armentrout sprinted off without another word.

"I don't get it, what made Baldwin sick?"

"We turned off the yaw damper and tried to induce oscillations that would make him airsick. It worked, but I hate to think what would have happened if his confederates had had a chance to take over. You guys have a story to tell," said Kevin.

Lights came on.

"Virginia State Police, nobody move. Everyone down on the ground, face down, spread legged."

The Virginia soil and grass smelled good to Kevin. Once the State Police sorted out who was who, this could all begin to be over.

13

LOBSTERS

As McLean Flynn said, "It was a fine soft night." Only it wasn't Ireland. It was seven thousand feet above the Appalachian Mountains.

"Washington Center, Lockheed 1108, now receiving White Sulphur VOR, request direct."

"Roger, Lockheed 1108, proceed direct SSU."

The needle on the number one NAV was slightly to the right of center, so John turned the heading bug a few degrees and the needle began to approach the center of the dial. He and 1108 had been aloft for a little more than four hours. Behind him were a thousand pounds of live Maine lobsters, destined for the Greenbrier resort at White Sulphur Springs.

The engines rumbled along. The night was just hazy enough above that he could make out only the brightest stars. The black blanket below held only scattered lights. Over the Jefferson National Forest, there is very little ground reference at night. Fifty miles ahead the beacon at Lewisburg swept the night, not yet in sight.

He tuned and identified the localizer at Greenbrier Valley Airport on the number one and switched the number two nav to SSU. The GPS said thirty five nautical to LWB.

Then they hit something. Everything went black. Wind roared. He couldn't see. He felt some pain in his face and eyes. He was still conscious. But he couldn't see!

His headset was gone. His face felt wet and sticky. There was a smell of flesh and blood and vomit, he thought.

He reached for the auxiliary mike below the panel. He could hear the speaker pop when he keyed the old carbon mike.

"Washington center, 1108 has had a midair with something. Pilot is blind. Windshield broken. Declaring an emergency."

"Roger, 1108. Still just one soul on board? Say fuel available."

John coughed and blew his nose. He was covered with a sticky fluid and his nose was clogged with it. He still couldn't see anything.

"Still just one soul on board, two hours of fuel, Washington."

"Roger, 1108."

Eleven oh eight was a Lockheed 12A. John and Dick had bought it from Oscar Tate when he retired it from Greenbrier Airlines. They needed a large twin with good range to go to Aroostook, Maine once a week to fly in fresh lobsters for the resort. Just as often, they flew to Rappahannock Bay or Mobjack Bay for oysters in season or other fresh fish. Fish once caught will remain edible for several days if properly refrigerated, but it will taste fresh for only a short time and will lose its precious edge if frozen.

It had been profitable enough, but it had been more fun than work for them. Their other ventures, centered on their ownership of the fixed base operation at LWB, kept them involved in flying even though they were both old enough to let others do it.

Now this!

"Washington, I cannot see a thing. I am afraid to touch my eyes for fear of making my injury worse. I want to try to contact my brother on unicom at Lewisburg."

"Frequency change approved, 1108. We are standing by. If you don't come back to us by radio, please call once you are on the ground."

"Roger, Washington, thanks."

"Lewisburg unicom, Lewisburg unicom, Lockheed 1108."

The radio crackled in the hangar. R.D. was under the Conquest II checking the oil reservoir on the right engine. He knew from the tone of his brother's voice that there was a problem.

He ran to the bench where the mike was.

"John, what's up?" he asked.

"I have had a midair with something. I am covered with blood, I think, some mine, some from something else. I can't see a thing. My last known position was thirty miles northeast of Lewisburg."

R.D. ran to the open door of the hangar. He could hear the Lockheed approaching.

"I can hear you, you are close to the field. Can you turn on your landing lights?"

"I'll try," said John.

The cord on the mike allowed R.D. to stand just outside of the hangar. He ran back ten feet to get his hand held transceiver and sprinted back to the open door.

"Can you hear me on this transmitter?"

"Yes," said John, "not quite a loud as the other, but I hear you."

R.D. said. "The tower is closed, but the localizer and glide slope are on. Maybe we can get you home that way."

"I cannot see the panel," said John.

"Are you on autopilot?" asked R.D.

"Affirmative," said John.

"Good, stand by." Long seconds passed as R.D. thought.

As he looked up into the night, he saw the landing lights of the Lockheed about two miles northeast of the field.

"I see you. I see you," R.D. said into the mic.

"Roger, good deal," said John.

"Can you turn using the heading bug?" asked R.D.

"Let me try," said John. "Everything is covered with sticky stuff. Smells like barf."

He reached up to the panel and turned the heading bug knob a little. The Lockheed gracefully turned a few degrees to the right. Then he turned it a little to the left. Same sweet response. Good old plane.

"The heading bug works. Now what?"

""What was your cruising altitude?" R.D. asked.

"Seven thousand."

"Good, you can clear any mountain within your fuel range. I want you to turn a little to the right, so I can bring you back on a teardrop turn to the localizer. I am going out to the center of the runway. "

As he ran, he broadcast: "All traffic in vicinity of Greenbrier Valley Airport, we have an emergency. Please do not transmit on this frequency until further advised."

"John, I still see you. Turn now about ten degrees to your right, and pull back power for a descent."

"Roger," said John.

R.D. could see the big twin respond. He showed his flashlight on his watch. Ten twenty five PM. He waited three minutes.

"John, I want you to turn now to approximate the localizer. You need to turn left a total of about two hundred ten degrees. Leave the plane on autopilot for now."

"Roger," said John. "Tell me when I have turned enough," and he turned the heading bug to begin the turn. As soon as he felt the plane begin to level from that turn, he turned the heading bug again.

"Let's see, about twenty degrees per adjustment, ten adjustments."

"How am I doing, bro?" he asked into the mic.

"O.K., keep turning, you have about sixty degrees to go."

The Lockheed kept up the blind waltz through the night.

"O.K., now you are close to the right heading," said R.D. "I am on the center stripe of the runway, have you in sight. You look about nine miles out. Slow up, but be careful. Do you know the throttle positions for about fifteen inches of manifold pressure?"

"I think so. I have been flying this plane so much, I think I can judge when I am at approach speed throttle settings."

"Good. When you have slowed to approach speed, drop your gear."

Long seconds passed. Still the twin lights bore toward R.D. on the runway.

"I think we are at approach speed now, lowering the gear."

"Don't make any elevator trim adjustments just yet," said R.D. "Let's see how you look when you get a little closer."

"O.K." said John. "If I don't make it, you take care of things, understand?"

"I understand, but you are going to make it O.K. I am looking right at you now. You look four miles out. Try flaps ten, now."

The lights wavered as the Lockheed nosed up with the flap application. Then the settled down and looked straight at R.D. again.

"Pull off a little more throttle, just a little, and turn right just a bit."

"Roger, little less power, right just a touch."

"Looks good, keep coming. You look about a thousand above the runway now."

"Roger," said John.

"Add just a little power, bro."

"Roger, just a little power."

"Looks good. Is your gear down?"

"I can't see anything, I felt that it went down, I heard the gear motor, but I cannot be sure it is locked."

"Feel the green lights," said R.D. "Are they hot?"

"Yes," came the reply after a few seconds.

"Then don't worry about the gear. And a little to the left now. You look about one mile out."

"She feels steady, just fly me to the runway," said John.

"O.K., keep coming. When you touch down, let her roll as straight as you can. Don't get on the brakes too hard. We have lots of flat land, no obstacles."

"Roger," said John. "What if I bounce?"

"Don't do that," said R.D. "Just do what I tell you."

"O.K. bro," came the response.

"Alignment looks good. Take off a little power. Half a mile now."

The twin lights looked so big in the night. When they are coming straight at you, they look so big.

"Two hundred yards to the threshold, now. Pull off a little more power and trim up just a touch."

"Roger," said John.

"Put back half of the power you took off," said R.D.

"Roger," said John.

"Looks good, bro. Fifty feet above the runway. Just fly her down."

"Roger," said John.

"O.K., pull off most of the power, you are ten feet above the runway. Flare just a little."

"O.K." said John.

The big twin touched down softly. R.D. heard John pull off the last of the power. He could hear the hiss of the brakes as the plane went past him. He had run to the edge of the runway to get out of the way, but now he trotted toward the rapidly decelerating plane.

The Lockheed came to a stop with one wheel just off the edge of the runway. It took R.D. almost two minutes to get there. When he opened the door, he knew immediately that the plane had hit a large bird. There were feathers and guts everywhere on top of the cartons of lobster.

He made his way to the front and gently helped his brother from the plane.

14

LEWISBURG

The first thing John saw when he opened his eyes was a field of daisies. It only took a minute for him to recall that he had pitched his tent behind the wing of N5611 B at Hinton Alderson Airport on the banks of the Greenbrier River. As he stretched and got out of the tent, the other fellows in his EAA Chapter were awakening. The morning fog hung heavily in the river valley. The smell of bacon cooking was in the air. He could see down toward the hangar there was already a small knot of people standing next to the grill. Thin blue smoke wafted up into the fog from the grill. He pulled on his jeans and stood up. Six planes were pushed back into the deep grass and daisies on the south side of the runway. It looked like they were peeking out of the woods. Even the big Stearman looked partially concealed.

At breakfast, they decided to fly over to Greenbrier Valley airport for fuel before returning to Robert

Newlon field. The prospect of a day of pleasure flying over the green hills was a nice thought.

The fog lifted quickly as the morning sun began to heat the valley to its fall normal temperature. By eight thirty, they were all fed and ready to depart for a day of flying. All six were to go to Greenbrier Valley airport. A Baby Ace, three one fifty's, a Star duster, John's 182 and the Stearman. They departed the grass strip toward the west and then made the turn around the mountain and laced back to follow the river upstream. The burnish of autumn colors had just started to turn the leaves. Bits of gold and red shown from the green hillsides. He throttled back to keep pace with the slower planes. His buddy Kevin Gallagher in the right seat swiveled his neck back and forth to take in the sights. Six planes in a chain up the river. What a great day. Over Ronceverte, they broke off toward the North. In a few minutes, they could see the seven thousand foot long runway 4 at Greenbrier Valley.

"Greenbrier Valley Tower, Cessna 5611 Bravo, flight of six, ten miles south, landing Lewisburg."

"Cessna 5611 Bravo, good morning, expect Runway 22, altimeter is three zero zero eight, wind in two four zero at six. Report entering left downwind."

"Roger, Lewisburg Tower, 5611 Bravo."

The lush valley opened up wider. Great place for an airport, he thought. Past the south end of the runway, with the threshold on his left, he called the tower.

"Tower, 5611 Bravo, flight of six, left downwind for Runway 22."

"5611 Bravo, flight of six, cleared to land."

"Roger, Tower, wish Chuck and Oscar Tate could join us. God bless their souls."

"Roger that, 5611 Bravo."

He pulled on a notch of flaps and slowed to eighty miles per hour on the base leg. A beautiful morning for flying.

In rapid succession, the six landed. As they taxied up to the ramp there was a group of people gathered around a Cessna Citation. All six lined up and shut down. They quickly tied down and walked over to the Citation. A man in a white smock and trousers seemed to be agitated. His arm movements telegraphed upset. As his group walked up, John and the others got their first clue of the source of trouble. The front tire on the Citation was flat. Small problem, he thought. Then he saw that the radome was fractured and a diamond shaped piece was missing.

Except for friendly nods, John and his people didn't speak. It became clear very quickly that this was more than just a flat tire situation. On the ramp beside the man in white was a large cooler, taped shut. Frost covered its middle. The man with the man in white said to the pilots, "This heart and lungs must be in Charleston immediately, can't you take off with a flat tire?"

"No, sir," said the older pilot. "We will just have to wait until we can get a mechanic here to fix it."

"How long will that take?" he asked the line man.

"This is Sunday. Even if I can reach him, which I doubt, he teaches Sunday school and won't want to miss."

"But a life hangs on time here," said the man in white. "If we cannot get this heart and lungs to Charleston, it will become untransplantable due to the passage of time. Is there no other way to get there?

Think about that while I call Dr. Mantz at Charleston Area Medical Center."

He trotted off toward the office.

"Sure would like to help," said the lineman, "but this is a rural area, people have plans for Sunday. I will go try, but I don't think he is home. He walked fast back toward the terminal."

John and the others could see the man in white, obviously stressed, talking on the telephone.

He said just as John and the others came into earshot, "Don't put him under just yet. I will call you back in a few minutes."

"What happened to the Citation?" asked Forrest.

"Hit a deer on landing," was the response.

John and the others looked up and down the field. Several aircraft were tied down, but no pilots were in sight.

As the man in white walked up, John asked, "How quickly do you have to get the transplant tissues to Charleston?"

The doctor looked up, surprised at the interruption of his thoughts. He shot a look at this watch.

"If we don't start the surgery within an hour and twenty five minutes, these tissues will be timed out. There is a team of surgeons ready to go at Charleston Area Medical Center. The patient is prepped and ready to be anesthetized. I just don't know what to do," he said.

"What needs to go to Charleston beside that cooler?" asked John.

"Nothing really, I would like to go, but it's optional."

John looked at Kevin, Kevin ran to the gas truck without another word.

"We'll take you to Charleston. Get that stuff into that Cessna 182. Call your doctors. Tell them we estimate Charleston in an hour." The doctor broke into a full sprint to the telephone.

John walked hastily back to 5611 Bravo. He checked the tires, checked the oil and did a brief walk around. The fuel truck was through fueling before the doctor came back out. He ran up.

"They say OK if we can do in it in an hour."

"Let's go, then, "said John. They put the cooler in the seat behind the pilot. Kevin swung the door shut on his side as John called, "Clear," and cranked the motor. The engine caught with a chug and settled into a brief idle before John added throttle. He noticed the guys he flew in with at the fence line. He and Kevin managed a quick wave.

"Tower, 5611 Bravo, expedited departure please."

"Roger, 5611 Bravo, understand. Taxi to Runway 22, intersection departure approved, cleared for takeoff, good luck."

John checked the magnetos on the roll. At the intersection, he turned as sharply as the 182 would tolerate and began adding throttle. As the manifold pressure hit maximum, the plane broke ground and vaulted into the morning. Before he was one hundred feet aloft, he began a shallow turn to a heading of two seven zero. Climb was good in the crisp air. They soon leveled off at four thousand five hundred feet. He kept the throttle all the way in. The airspeed built to one sixty. He pulled the prop back to twenty four hundred fifty and leaned the mixture some.

He spun the dial on the radio. "Charleston Radio, Charleston Radio, Cessna 5611 Bravo, off Greenbrier Valley, calling on 116.6."

You could almost smell the coffee as they imagined the Specialist walking over to the console. Then came, "5611 Bravo, this is Charleston Radio, go ahead."

"Charleston, 5611 Bravo, off Greenbrier Valley, level at four thousand five hundred, cannot reach Charleston Approach at this distance. We have an emergency other than with the aircraft. We have on board a heart and lung transplant enroute to Charleston Area Medical Center. Time is critical. Please call Approach and ask for expedited handling for us into Charleston. We are guarding 124.1 and will call them as soon as possible. Personnel are standing by to pick up the transplant tissues, we understand."

"Roger, 5611 Bravo, stand by."

By this time, they were over the bridge on the New River gorge. Tourists were already stopping to get the view. They flew on.

"5611 Bravo, Charleston Approach."

"Charleston Approach, 5611 Bravo, go ahead."

"5611 Bravo, squawk four zero one one and ident, please."

In a minute, he said, "Radar contact, 5611 Bravo. Say airspeed."

"Airspeed, indicated, is one five two miles per hour."

"5611 Bravo, we show your ground speed is one thirty, suggest you descend to increase speed. Winds aloft forecast for east of Charleston at three thousand AGL is 207 at one six knots."

"Roger, Charleston, we will descend."

"If we lose you on radar, be advised we are giving you expedited handling and will be standing by when we pick you up again."

John and Kevin had descended to three thousand feet by now. They couldn't tell, but they had picked up eight miles per hour ground speed. As they topped the next ridge about ten miles from where they reached three thousand feet, they reacquired Charleston Approach.

"5611 Bravo, Charleston Approach."

"Charleston Approach, 5611 Bravo back with you, level now at three thousand. We are three six zero from Beckley VOR."

"Roger, 5611 Bravo. While you were off the air, Charleston Area Medical Center called. The time is critical. They will begin the surgery in anticipation of arrival of the transplant. Minutes are critical, they say. They have a police car standing by at Yeager field, but they ask if you could land closer to the hospital."

"5611 Bravo. We will land anywhere they want us to, but what field closer than Yeager?"

"Stand by, 5611 Bravo, I have one of the doctors on the land line."

Minutes passed. The Belle Island airport appeared in the Kanawha River. They swept over without looking down. All eyes in the plane were focused on what lay ahead. The city of Charleston lay in the river valley ahead. Both pilots were involuntarily leaning forward in their seats. Kevin tapped John on the arm.

"Take a break," he said. "Relax a minute. You can't push this plane any faster than the engine."

"Thanks," said John and let himself slump back into the seat. He could feel the tension in his trunk subside as he relaxed a bit in the seat. "Starkeeper, stay with us," he said.

Kevin heard in his headsets. He gave John an affirmative look, and a thumbs up.

"5611 Bravo, Charleston Approach."

"Go ahead Approach."

"One of the assistant surgeons is a pilot. He said to ask you if you would land on Kanawha Boulevard. It's only three blocks from the hospital. It would save ten minutes at least."

"Stand by Charleston," said John.

He looked over at Kevin. His expression said, "What do you think?"

Kevin thought for a few seconds and said, "Tell them yes."

"Charleston Approach, 5611 Bravo can land on Kanawha Boulevard. Please clear traffic."

Roger, 5611 Bravo, Charleston Police are on it now. We will report Boulevard secure. How is your situation?"

"We are fine. Plenty of fuel, no problems. What kind of a person is the transplant for?"

"We understand he is a thirty two year old father of four."

"Roger," said John.

"Better begin your descent, five six one one bravo."

"Roger, five six one one bravo out of three thousand for one thousand, following the river."

As they rounded a bend in the river, they could see the Capitol. Just beyond it, the road was speckled with flashing lights.

"This could be touchy, "said John.

"Yes, luckily the power lines are on the side away from the river," said Kevin. "Everybody should have eyes peeled for wires as we descend," he said.

"Sure enough," said John and pulled off some power. They kept to the middle of the river until they passed the Capitol.

"Never saw so many police cars," John said.

"Lots of them, aren't there?" Said Kevin.

John pulled off more throttle, pulled on a first notch of flaps and waited for the 182 to slow.

"Wow, this is really something, isn't it?" he said to Kevin.

"Watch closely, take the yoke if I falter or mess up, OK?"

"You're doing fine. Let's carry the mail."

He shot a glance at the doctor in the back seat, then told him to cinch his seatbelt tight.

At six hundred fifty feet and eighty miles per hour, John began to swing the plane toward the north bank. Police cars as far as he could see had every street blocked onto the Boulevard. Cars were up on the curbs on the north side. Plenty of room, he thought as he swung close. Now on short final, then the plane settled onto the concrete. As soon as he did, the police car behind him began to follow.

John pulled the mixture as they swept to a stop. The doctor leaped out and snagged the cooler behind him. Before Kevin and John could get out, the doctor climbed into the cruiser with the cooler and it squealed away. Another cruiser ran interference for it as they sped north on Brooks Street.

John and Kevin got out. A cruiser came up and stopped. Out got an officer, another man in white, and a woman with a small child in her arms. John and Kevin met them half way between the plane and the car.

"You guys OK?" asked the officer.

"Couldn't be better," said Kevin.

"This is Mrs. Adkins," said the officer. "She wanted to meet you both."

Mrs. Adkins was crying and clutching her child. She couldn't speak. John and Kevin nodded their understanding. Their eyes filled too. Finally, she choked out "Thank you." It was all she could do. The officer helped her back into the car and they went away onto Brooks Street.

Suddenly, Kevin and John realized that they were relatively alone, here on Kanawha Boulevard, on Sunday morning, just as churches were being let out. The side streets were full. People seemed to know what was happening.

The officer asked, "Which way do you want to take off?"

John said, "We'll taxi back toward the Capitol and take off to the west."

There had certainly been lots of bigger parades down the Boulevard in Charleston, but probably none happier than that little Cessna with a police car in front and behind as it taxied back up toward the Capitol. People waved and honked. At the end of the cleared area, the first car pulled off to the side to give them room to turn around. The officers all saluted as they turned the Cessna into the wind and opened the throttle.

15

THE ISLAND

There were still wisps of fog in the morning air as Ernie flared the Cessna 195 in the grass at Newlon Field. This morning had been all summer coming. The whole club had turned out during the week to fix things for the fly-in breakfast. Danny and Joy were already cooking patties of sausage on the camp stove. The field was gathering its flock. The variety of aircraft already there because they were based there or which had already arrived ran from single seat Baby Ace's to light twins.

If you wanted pancakes, you got in line and put in your donation. Soon you would be served a Styrofoam plate with a stack of three and two packs of "maple syrup" and butter. The smell of coffee permeated the air that wasn't already permeated with the smell of sausage. It was a happy time. By eight o'clock, there were probably fifty souls there and the pleasant din of multiple conversations filled the air.

Just as the aircraft were of a wide variety, so were the participants. The only thing that bound them together was love of airplanes. Ages ran from seventeen to seventy five. Then Ross Taylor walked in. He looked gaunt. Just a year before, he had suffered a serious heart attack. Everyone was concerned for him and his family. He was warmly greeted by all. Before he and his wife got in line for their pancakes and sausage, they drifted to the back of the hangar to talk with Jimmy Burdette who was putting the finishing touches on a Stearman restoration.

The old black dial-type telephone on the barrel in the corner rang. Ross answered it.

"No," he said, "We drove down last night," he said into the phone.

"How do you know?" he asked.

"How long to they think you have?" he asked.

"How many pilots do you need?" he asked.

"How many people must be evacuated?" he asked.

"Stay by the phone. I will call you back in ten minutes," he said.

He walked purposefully to the open door of the hangar, which put him at the edge of the crowd.

He said, "Hey folks, can I have your attention for a minute?"

Everyone turned to hear him. It got quiet very quickly. You could hear the sausage sizzling.

"We have a problem. That telephone call was from Sam Meads. While we slept last night, there was a big rainstorm over Greenbrier County and Fayette County. There have been flash floods all down the Greenbrier River Valley and in the New River Valley. The water is supposed to crest in Belle, West Virginia at two feet over flood stage by ten o'clock this morning. Sam and Denny have ten airplanes at Belle Island Airport that have to be flown out immediately if they are to be saved. There are also six people trapped by water on the island who need to be evacuated. The National Guard Helicopters are all up in Greenbrier County and Fayette County rescuing stranded victims of the flood."

"You have the situation. Now elect a leader and get Sam some help. I will help, but I need to be careful."

"Who will take over?" asked one of the women.

John said, "Ernie, you have the most landings at Belle Island airport in this crowd. You know what planes are up there and you are the closest to Sam in the group. You lead."

Everyone quickly agreed.

Ernie came forward.

"How many of you are able to go as pilots of your planes? We need eight pilots in addition to those who fly us up there. Denny and Sam can each fly one plane out. If we fly four of our four seaters up there, we can take two extra pilots in each plane. While you are thinking about it, consider this. There are two Baby Aces. No one should fly them except experienced tail dragger pilots. Denny will take one of them. There is a Cessna 150/150, anyone current in a 150 or 152 could fly that out. There are two 172s. Sam will fly out the 182. There are three Cherokees, two are hundred fifty horse, and one is one eighty horse. Then, there is the Lockheed 12. I have a cylinder from the left engine in my shop. Mike, you take over, Jimmy and I will sprint to my shop and pick up the cylinder and meet you as soon as possible at Lawrence County."

Quickly Mike Mealey stepped forward. Mike was a CFI and had been a loadmaster in Viet Nam. His usually jovial manner turned serious.

"First question, I need four aircraft with pilots willing to land at Belle. Remember, it's short, only fourteen hundred feet, wet on both ends. I need eight pilots who are willing to go with those pilots and fly out the trapped airplanes.

"OK, first of all which planes will we take?"

"I'll go," said Al. That brought a Cherokee 180 and an instrument rated pilot into the group.

"Me, too," said Dee. "If someone will loan me a plane, I will fly up there. I have six landings at Belle."

"You can take my XP," said Ross.

"Who else?"

"I don't know if I can get my plane stopped," said George.

"Nonsense," said John, "you make the best trimmed landings of any of us."

"Well, OK, if you believe in me, I'll go."

"I'll go in with Mike in the 182," said John. "Now how many do we have?"

"Four planes, five pilots."

"Count Ernie and Jimmy, that makes seven," some one said.

"We need three more."

"Danny will go," said Joy. "I will finish the cooking."

"We need two more."

Things got quiet again.

"If you can get me in there, I reckon I can get myself out," said Forrest Burdette.

The group got quiet again.

Rick Akers and his wife arrived.

Quickly Mike told them about Sam's problem.

"You go, Richard," she said. "We'll save the pancake batter for a late lunch."

He smiled. We had our crew.

"OK, here is the plan. John and I will go in 5611 Bravo. We will pick up Ernie and Jimmy at Lawrence County and catch up with you guys at Belle. Break up into groups. Take a light fuel load if you can. Fly the planes to Charleston. We'll meet there after. Now go!"

Mike and John sprinted to 5611 Bravo. They shared the pre-flight inspection. Mike yelled "Clear" and engaged the starter just as John swung into the right seat. 5611 Bravo had been tied down next to the hangar. Mike pulled straight out, checking the magnetos on the roll. He pulled on two notches of flaps and steadily pushed the throttle in.

"Newlon traffic, five six one one bravo, midfield take off on Runway 20 at Newlon," spoke John into the radio.

Both pilots knew they and the plane had just eleven hundred feet to the ditch at the end of the runway. The plane didn't even shrug about it. At about six hundred feet from the hangar, the nose wheel came out of the grass and the rest of 5611 Bravo followed shortly. Mike kept the yoke well back, but as soon as he was above the trees on the river bank, he lowered the nose to gain speed and pointed the nose directly at Lawrence County Airport, some ten miles ahead.

"Huntington Approach, Cessna Skylane 5611 Bravo, off Newlon, going to Lawrence County, squawking twelve hundred."

"Good Morning 5611 Bravo, Huntington Approach, squawk 3022 and ident."

"Pat is that you?" said Mike.

"Yeah, they got me up here rather than at the fly-in. Got to work until eleven. Say, how come you guys are flying and not eating pancakes?"

"Sam Meads called a few minutes ago. Seems like there was a big rain up the valley last night. The Weather people expect the water to flood Belle Island Airport in two hours. We are flying four airplanes up there with eight pilots to fly out the trapped airplanes. We are going to Lawrence County to pick up Ernie and Jimmy with a cylinder for the Lockheed 12."

"Wow, you guys have your hands full," said Pat. "I will call Charleston on the land line and advise your plans. They can give you a vector through their airspace direct to Belle Island."

"Thanks, Pat, we have Lawrence County in sight," said John.

"Frequency change approved, see you later," said Pat.

"Roger," said John and flipped the radio switch to unicom for Lawrence County.

Jimmy and Ernie were waiting by the runway, each with a large bag of tools and what they could carry. Mike touched down just past the numbers and stopped smoothly. Jimmy and Ernie ran up the last few yards from where they were waiting and boarded. No time to put stuff in the luggage compartment, they held their tools and airplane parts on their laps. Since they were about mid-field, Mike just turned around and pushed in the throttle.

"Lawrence County traffic, Skylane 5611 Bravo is departing Runway 26 midfield." The big engine pulled and 5611 Bravo ate up the runway. A hundred feet short of the numbers, it swung its nose upward. The prop wash pushed the tall grass at the end of the runway back as they roared past.

"Who is that guy you are always talking about that watches over airplanes?" asked Mike.

"Starkeeper," murmured John.

"Ask him to watch out for us."

"Roger," said John. They exchanged a look.

"Huntington Approach, Skylane 5611 Bravo, squawking twelve again."

"5611 Bravo, Huntington Approach. I called Charleston Approach. They will vector you directly to Belle. Your buddies took off in a stream about eight minutes ago. They are over Milton at three thousand. They said to tell you that they are guarding 123.3. "

"Roger, Pat, thanks. Leaving the frequency now, but we will monitor you. Call if you need us to change course or something."

"Roger, Good luck," said Pat.

With the radio now set to 123.3, John said "Cherokee 1681 Papa, do you read 5611 Bravo?"

"Read you loud and clear, 5611 Bravo, go ahead."

"Where are you guys?" asked John.

"Just over the Nitro Interstate Bridge, at three thousand feet. Charleston gave us a vector of one one eight degrees. Will you catch up or go separately? '"

"We will get our own vector," said John, Stand by."

"Charleston Approach, Skylane 5611 Bravo."

"5611 Bravo, Charleston Approach, good morning."

"Good Morning, Charleston, 5611 Bravo is going with the other aircraft to Belle Island Airport, request direct vector and expedited handling."

"Roger," said Charleston, "stand by." Seconds passed. Then, "5611 Bravo, fly heading one one zero degrees. Be advised, Sam Meads called us just twenty minutes ago to alert us to your flight. He said the water is within two feet of covering the ends of the runway. Do you think you can get in and out in time?"

"We have to try, Charleston Approach. The really critical thing is that we have to replace a cylinder on the Lockheed 12 before it can be flown out. We plan to be the last plane off."

"Well, we are all pulling for you guys. Let us know if we can do anything to help."

"Roger, Charleston, and thanks. If you approve, we will use 123.3 for communications between members of this flight and we will monitor your frequency 124.1. "

"That is approved, five six one one bravo. Call us if you need to."

"Cherokee 1681 Papa, we are just passing over the TV tower, where are you guys?"

"We are parallel with the Patrick Street Bridge. I think you can catch us before we land. "

"Any problems?"

"No, everyone is fine. How do you want this to go, Mike?"

"Let's let the more experienced pilots land first. The rest of you watch closely. Use short field technique. Put it down in the first fifty feet or go around. Stay off the brakes until landing roll is stabilized. Landing order will be me, Al, Rick and George. Any questions? Acknowledge!"

"Mike, this is Rick. Plan is OK, we are ready."

"Mike, this is Al. We are OK with your plan."

"Mike, this is George. Forest says he will stick his foot out to help brake if we need him to." Nobody spoke. Forest was seventy five years old. They all loved him and secretly dreaded the day he would leave them.

"We have you in sight," said John.

"Where?" said Mike.

"Twelve thirty and six miles."

"Oh, yeah, I got them," said Mike.

"Sam, do you hear us on 123.3?" asked John.

"Hear you loud and clear," said Sam.

"What is your situation?" John asked.

"Not much change. Water about one foot from upriver end of runway. We pre-flighted and started all the planes. They should be no problem once you guys get here. The Lockheed is rolled out, right engine started and warmed up. Cowl is off the left engine. Denny and I will stay to help with the cylinder. What is your situation?"

"We have eight pilots for you. No problems to report. They are holding the pancakes for us at Newlon, but we plan to reconnoiter at Charleston airport. We have you in sight, Sam. We will be landing upriver."

"Sure is a pretty sight. We'll monitor the radio."

"OK," said Mike, "here we come."

By this time, they had all descended to sixteen hundred feet, just even with the tops of the hills lining the Kanawha River. They all flew by on the right to get a look at the runway and the water.

"Wow, look at that," said Mike, "Looks like an aircraft carrier."

"Wish we had their arresting gear," said George.

"OK, guys, space out your downwinds so everyone has plenty of time to get off the runway."

"How much do you think we need?" asked Al.

"Count twenty seconds before you turn base after the guy in front of you turns."

With that they began their cross wind leg over the river.

On downwind, Mike dropped below the hill to his right and began configuring 5611 Bravo for slow flight. As he turned final, about two thousand feet from the threshold, his altitude was seven hundred fifty MSL, just two hundred feet above the runway. His airspeed was sixty. Occasionally the stall warning buzzed. If there had been numbers in the grass at Belle, five six one one bravo would have touched them as it arrived. As soon as the mains touched, Mike eased onto the brakes and released all the flaps. 5611 Bravo was now definitely on the ground. As soon as the airspeed got down to forty five, Mike again put on full flaps. The big panels helped the braking as he brought them to a stop a good hundred yards from the far end. He quickly turned the plane around and gave it some throttle to taxi back to the hangar as Al came down final the last two hundred feet. Mike stopped fifty feet from Sam. As they got out, Al went by heavy on the brakes, in good shape. As Sam and the rest watched, Rick brought the spare 172 in. Right on the numbers, good speed.

"Now let's get George in."

Just like always, George had the trim set for a lot of nose up. He had plenty of power on and looked good. At fifty feet from touch down, he eased out the throttle and his plane settled into the grass in good shape.

Now they were all there. Sam assigned planes to the eight pilots. They ran for their planes and made ready. Jimmy, Ernie and John ran to N1108, the old Lockheed

12. Jimmy had been assigned the Baby Ace and Ernie the 150/150. Both were ready and warmed up and sat near the Lockheed.

Jimmy quickly set a stepladder beside the left engine. Carefully, Ernie unwrapped the cylinder. With three of them to steady it, they lifted it up to the right position. Jimmy pushed in the wrist pin and the connecting rod was attached to the piston. Next, they pushed the cylinder over the rest of the piston and down onto the lugs in the crankcase. Jimmy spun nuts on his side and John did his side. Ernie began connecting the exhaust header. Two nuts to tighten and it was done. The intake manifold was next, then the spark plug leads, front and back.

"The water is three inches below the end of the runway up there," said Denny, his face flushed from the run back.

"I figure we have twenty minutes to roll or give up. How is it coming?"

"I think we can do it," said Ernie. "John, preflight and get in the pilot's seat. This is going to be close."

The first plane to take off roared by, getting airborne at just two thirds of the runway. Next the other Baby Ace went by, easily airborne before half of the runway. Dried grass fragments created a cloud around them. John swung through the aft door of the Lockheed.

"How is the battery, Sam?" asked John.

"Should be OK," said Sam. "If it won't start, we'll have to leave it. Sure would be a shame."

"Primer line is on. Jimmy, check me here, is this all we need to do?" asked Ernie.

"Let's see, exhaust, intake, primer, spark plug wires, base nuts torqued. Looks good. I say we turn it over.

Once is starts, each of us dash for our planes and get out of here."

Sam and Denny nodded and hustled over to their planes.

"Clear," shouted John and pushed the right starter button. The 450 Pratt and Whitney belched a cloud of light blue smoke and came to life. Without waiting for it to settle down, John pushed the starter button for the left engine, priming as he did. Blades went by the side window of the cockpit. Six, eight, ten. John stopped cranking, primed some more, counted to ten and cranked it again. This time, it caught, rough and smoky. No cowling, he thought, I wonder how that will affect the flying characteristics?

Now that he could see the oil pressure coming up, he eased the throttles up a bit and began to turn toward the upriver end of the runway. The twin tail dragger eased through the grass with dignity.

"There goes Jimmy. Here comes Ernie."

Now he was the last. He could see planes flying the pattern, everybody waiting to see if everyone made it off.

As he reached the north end of the runway, the last fifty feet of it were under water. He taxied as far as he dared and turned the Lockheed toward the south end of the runway.

Let's see, lightly loaded, I'll start with no flaps and pop them on about half way down the runway, he thought. He ran the right engine up. No problems. Magnetos checked, OK. Left engine run-up. Little shaky. Lean those wet plugs! Now smooth. Full throttle on both. Lots of noise. Grass flew. He let off the brakes and the big twin surged ahead. As he passed the hangars at the half way point, he pushed the flap lever all the way down. The flaps seemed to levitate the big plane in just a few seconds, but it was just a hundred feet from the end of the runway when it lifted off. John slowly milked off half of the flaps and stabilized the airspeed at ninety for the climb. As he gently climbed up between the mountains, he retracted the landing gear.

"Thanks, Starkeeper, we needed you today."

He said into the mic. "Newlon flight, I smell pancakes."

16

SARAJEVO

The moment the telephone rang, John wished that he had moved it off of the side table beside the bed. He and Susan were instantly wide awake. He found the telephone by feel, since he came to it before he located the line switch for the light. The dim light from beneath the door was simply not enough to guide him, so he answered the telephone in the dark.

"John, this is Kevin."

"I might have known! What is it? Where are you?"

"I'm in Crete," came the loud but scratchy reply. "I need some help. Are you and Susan planning to go home tomorrow?"

"Yes, we are flying to London, then riding the night flight from Gatwick to Newark."

"Before I tell you what I want, let me say that if you will help us, we can get you and Susan tickets on Concorde to Kennedy. Airline people are being most cooperative."

"OK, I'm properly impressed, now what awful thing must I do to get the prize?"

"There is a group of school children, sons and daughters of diplomatic personnel who were enroute to England from various points in what used to be Yugoslavia now in Sarajevo. While the students were being rounded up, the Foreign Service evacuated the parents on an earlier flight before the Serbs grabbed the airport. The Serbs took several pilots prisoner, including ours for the evacuation flight, at the Sarajevo airport. Now, it seems that the Croats have retaken the airport temporarily and the plane, a C-54 belonging to the Red Cross is ready to go, but no pilots. The situation is unstable in the max. Our airline has diverted a couple of pilots to take our 747 on to Kennedy from Athens, but Nicholas Ashley-Cox and I are the only C-54 qualified pilots they could scrape up on short notice. He and I have volunteered to go to Sarajevo and fly the C-54 to England."

"That's really good of you, Kevin, I'm proud of you, partner. But, if you have pilots, why the call? '"

"There's just one additional teeny weeny problem," said Kevin.

"Sure, sure. I don't like the sound of this. Better get it over with."

"As you might suspect, this time of the year, all of Europe is socked in, from about two hundred miles west of Sarajevo to the east coast of England, but the air is clear above eight thousand feet. The other problem you asked about is the reason for my call."

He hesitated. John waited a few seconds.

Kevin resumed, "The two U.N. contract pilots were captured by the Serbs. They were to fly four adoptive babies out of Sarajevo to England tonight. Their plane, a Charlie model Aztec like ours is gassed up and waiting at the airport in Sarajevo. The children are at a U.N. facility near the airport. These children are orphans and their adoption by British couples has been arranged through a U. N. agency. If the children are captured by the Serbs, they will disappear like others have. I want you to fly the Aztec to England."

There was a long silence.

"I don't know what to say, Kevin. You are going to have to hold while I bring Susan up to date on this."

Kevin said he would hold.

John left the telephone receiver uncovered so Kevin could hear him tell Susan about the situation.

"Can't they get someone else?" she asked.

"Kevin, can't they get someone else?" John asked.

"I've tried every way I know how. If Lois hadn't remembered that you two had reservations to spend the last four days of your vacation at the Metropole in Piraeus, we wouldn't have found you. We Methodists stick together, you know."

"Wait till I get a chance to tell her how grateful we are to her," said Susan into the telephone. She was now holding her ear next to the earpiece with John.

"Kevin, we need to talk about this. Call us back in ten minutes."

"OK, will do." The call terminated.

"If we decided to do this crazy thing, how soon could we leave the Hotel?" asked John.

"I could be packed in twenty minutes. But do you really want to do this? Can you do it? "

"Can *I* do it?" He asked. "I need someone to manage four infants in an Aztec. He meant both of us."

"You and your flying friends get into some of the most bizarre situations. Do you and he try to think up something more weird than the last time as some sort of game or something? This beats anything yet! You expect me to get out of a warm bed, with the prospect of a perfect sunrise beaming into our beautiful room overlooking a picture postcard harbor in one of the most scenic and romantic spots on Earth, leave in the middle of the night, and somehow be transported to a war zone to retrieve a stranded Aztec with four infants to care for on a cloudy night and fly a thousand miles to England, over mountains, cold mountains, in a strange plane?"

"I don't expect you to do it. I just think we ought to consider how much those people need help. Innocent people are being killed. Parents in England are panic stricken over their stranded children. It is a chance to do something really worthwhile for someone who can never repay us. WWJD?"

"I suppose, He would say, 'Come, follow me,' and He would see that you got on your way."

"I'm not being sarcastic, I just feel that you and I have had an abundant life. We have felt helpless only a few times, just enough to know the feeling. I won't go if you don't want me to."

"I don't want you to go without me," she said.

"What if one of those children was Truman or Clara?" he asked. That did it.

She found the light switch and was under way in one smooth motion. The questions were answered. They were packed and ready to go when Kevin called back.

"Bless you both for doing this," he said.

"How do we get from here to there?"

"The U.N. has rented a PBY Catalina from an oceanographic survey company. They are going to fly in a supply of medical stuff and emergency rations and water. We can take off immediately and land just south of Piraeus at the Greek Navy Base. We can be there in an hour and twenty minutes. "

"We'll be waiting for you," said Susan.

The Catalina was the same color as the clouds. It materialized rather than appeared. Then its landing lights came on as a warning to any itinerant boatman in its way. Any other time, they would have marveled at the sight, an early morning water landing of a big twin engine plane. Water flew up in great rooster tails as it first touched down. Then, as it decelerated, it settled quickly and just gushed water to the side. By the time it reached the dock area, with its great radial engines idling, John and Susan were in a boat handled by Greek sailors who put them alongside in professional style. John and Susan knew that the Greeks knew what was afoot. One of the men crossed himself as they thanked him and said goodbye.

As the boatswain signaled he was clear, the pilot began a turn to takeoff position. John and Susan were pointed to seats in the starboard blister. The first two hundred yards of the takeoff run seemed rough, like a boat in choppy water. Then, as the great plane hauled itself up onto the step, it smoothed out. More takeoff run. It seemed longer than a land takeoff. Then, with a surge, the Catalina came unglued from the water. Gracefully it roared into the sunrise. Then a left turn and the expedition left Piraeus to the north.

In a few minutes, Kevin came back to talk.

"Not much to tell in addition. Croats still hold Sarajevo. The airport is secure for now. Estimated time of arrival is two hours fifty minutes, about ten AM local. Get some sleep. I'm in the radioman's seat if you need me."

John signaled OK with his hand. He pulled an army blanket around Susan and they cuddled into the wide observer's seat. Somehow they managed to get some sleep.

The changing of the propellers pitch awakened them to the beginning of the descent. Kevin came back.

"Good news. Airport is still secure. We should be on the ground in ten minutes."

"Look at the size of that wheel," she said, as the landing gear came out in front of their blister.

"Looks like about five feet in diameter," John said.

Then they got their first look at Sarajevo. Steep hillsides, narrow valleys, some flat land. They flew through a narrowing valley and then it opened up to a wide, flat bottomed valley. The pilot made a right base to the runway and they lost sight of it as he turned final. The big tire yelped and produced a big chug of blue smoke as the Catalina planted itself. The pilot kept speed up until he was close to the place he wanted to stop as he didn't waste time or space. A group of about thirty troops and Red Cross personnel waited. As soon as the prop on his side stopped, John opened the blister hatch and he and Susan climbed down. Someone forward had opened the cargo hatch on the side and men were already passing boxes hand to hand to the trucks waiting.

A tall Red Cross nurse walked up to them.

"I am Marilyn Royce with the Red Cross. Thank goodness you have come. We need to get these children out of here. We have a hot meal waiting for you. Then we have arranged a met briefing through the U.N. military attaché. Your plane is in a hangar on the other side of the runway. I have a car waiting. "

They walked quickly. Just as John took hold of the door handle, a shell burst against a hillside about a mile away. He was surprised at how strong the shock wave was this far away. He gave Susan a look. She gave him a look, too.

"A Turkey dinner with all the trimmings. It seems that holiday food is the normal stuff that the Red Cross stocks," Marilyn said. "It sure tastes good, compared to some of the food we usually get."

"Are you usually stationed in Sarajevo?" asked Susan.

"No, I was assigned to a village in Kosovo province until this erupted. Our higher-ups told us to beat it here and be evacuated. We will go out as soon as the last of the U.S. civilians are out."

Another shell burst somewhere more distant than the earlier one.

"I'm Major Peterson," he said.

Squat, balding, but stout and capable, were the first thoughts John had as he looked up.

"I've come to give you a met briefing, such as we have. He spread a large chart on the table as they swept aside the paper plates."

"Due to the nature of the hostilities, we recommend that you exit the area to the south for about fifty miles, then turn on course. By that time, a heading of about two eight five should get you off to a good start. The bad news is that all of Europe is still fogged in. Once you head west, you will need to go to the English Channel to be able to see the ground. Your aircraft is equipped with long range tanks. One hundred ninety two gallons, all but eight usable. That should give you about six and one half hours range without reserve. What does the Aztec cruise at, Mr. Hache?"

"Book cruise speed at maximum gross weight is one hundred seventy eight knots, about two hundred six miles per hour."

"Then you should make it in about five hours, plus a little. I had our mechanics check the plane out since you cannot get a briefing from the intended pilots. It has just over five thousand hours total time. Right engine is six hundred since overhaul. Left engine is fifteen hundred. It seems fit and my men are guarding it until you leave."

"Thanks, Major, but how about our passengers?"

"I'll let Ms. Royce fill you in about that." He rose and turned to go.

John and Susan turned to Marilyn.

"The children range in age from six weeks to ten months. We have arranged a supply of diapers, formula, blankets, the usual baby supplies and stuff. As a precaution, we put a little Dramamine in their last formula. There is a bottle on board. I put a bottle of Phenobarbital in there too."

"Thanks, we may need that to calm them if the ride is bumpy," said Susan.

A car pulled up just as they came out. The lady driver said, "Well, here are your charges, come have a look."

The babies were all wrapped and blanketed like link sausages on the back seat of the old Ford. A Red Cross nurse was at the other door, checking another time to see if a change was called for.

The Aztec was U.S. Registry. N6322Y. Typical red, black and white Piper mid-sixties paint scheme. The paint looked original, and in good condition. As he walked around it, he thought of his own N5611B in the hangar in Nashville.

"You and I are a long way from home," he said, as he patted the left cowling.

The oil was up to the correct mark on the dipstick on both sides. The hydraulic reservoir was full. The tires were inflated right. Control surfaces checked good. The plane was ready. He got aboard. All of the charts and approach plates were in a leather bag behind the right seat, just within reach. The panel of radios was modern. A KX155, a KX170B, a King transponder, a Narco ADF. One of the military personnel had left a portable GPS in the right seat. It was camouflage colored, but the brand name of Magellan was clear. It had a cord for the cigar lighter. Everything looked OK.

The nurses and Red Cross workers came in with Susan. Four of them carried a baby each. A chaplain came with them. Susan got aboard in the middle row on the right. The ladies passed the babies up to Susan one at a time. She put them on the blanket covered back seats. Some thoughtful person had taken out the bulkhead between the passenger compartment and the aft luggage compartment. She could reach over the seats and get anything out of there she needed.

The chaplain said, "I know you are foreign to a war zone, but we have arranged a clearance for you to depart with a void time in fourteen minutes," as he consulted his watch.

"The base commander said for you to start up in the hangar, taxi as swiftly as you like, call tower during taxi, do not hesitate at the threshold." He paused as the noise of a departing plane drowned him out. Out the open door, John and Susan watched as the C-54 roared by two hundred yards away. Its nose gear lifted just as it passed them.

When the din had subsided, the Chaplain said, "Kevin said you and he were friends back stateside. He told me about the Starkeeper. I pray He stays with you for this flight. God bless you both."

He nodded to the nurses and they wasted no time departing.

For a moment, it was quiet. John and Susan gave each other a look. Commitment.

He pulled the starter switch for the left engine. It started easily and idled quietly, its propeller swishing by the open window. He started the right. It came up quickly too, and the oil pressures settled into the right place in their ranges. He turned on the radios and adjusted frequencies for the navigation aids, tower and approach.

"Sarajevo Tower, 6322Yankee taxiing to runway three two, request takeoff clearance."

It was just about a quarter mile to the threshold.

"You are cleared for takeoff 6322 Yankee, no delay at the threshold, left turn on departure, squawk 4033, altimeter setting three zero zero two, departure on 127.5."

"Thanks tower," he said and read back the numbers.

On the roll, he set the altimeter and the transponder and checked the magnetos. "OK, cowl flaps open, gear switch down, flaps up for takeoff, temperatures OK, door locked, trim set, props cycled, ready to go."

Just before he turned toward the runway threshold, he turned and gave Susan a quizzical look. "You ready?" he asked.

"Did you check everything?" she always asked. It was something they always did before a takeoff.

"Yes, I did," he said.

"Let's go, then," she said. Just after she spoke, a shell burst to the right of the midpoint of the runway.

"6322 Yankee, there appears no damage to the runway, but there is some debris on the right half of the runway. Use left half of runway and expedite departure."

"Roger, 6322 Yankee is rolling."

Down the runway they surged. Strong engines, pulling hard. He held the throttles up, even though they would have stayed up once set. It was a good hand position for takeoff. They roared into the late afternoon sky.

"Gear coming up," he thought. Next, he began a standard rate left turn. The whole of Sarajevo came into sight. Fires were burning all over town in a scattered pattern, or no pattern. He felt a pang of sorrow for the people below, who were forced to watch their homes destroyed.

"Stick with us, Starkeeper, we need your guiding hand today," he mumbled to himself. As he leveled the wings in the climb, he glanced back at Susan. Just as their eyes met, she began to turn to check on her charges.

In a minute they were in the clouds.

"Climb straight ahead, heading one niner zero," he thought.

"Up to ten thousand, that is where the met officer said we would be in the clear."

He watched the gauges closely. The autopilot was not to be used until he was in the clear above, so he could check it out, so he hand flew the Aztec up and up. Eight thousand, niner thousand, still in the soup. At ten, he began to detect a slight brightening and just above ten five, they broke into the clear.

"Not to worry about altitude," he thought. They had a block clearance and were on military radar. He would be depending on air traffic control to keep others away tonight. Minimal radio use was requested until they exited the "war zone," so he was surprised to hear Sarajevo call.

"6322 Yankee, Approach."

"Go ahead, Approach, 6322 Yankee," he said.

"Your friend Kevin has a problem. A flak burst on takeoff evidently got their wiring or batteries. No radio, no radio compass, no lights. Luckily the artificial horizon is vacuum operated. They reported incipient radio failure at eight thousand on a heading of one niner zero. They planned to fly another ten minutes in climb, then turn to heading of two eighty-five. Say your flight conditions."

"6322 Yankee is level ten five, between layers, good visibility, temperature six, smooth ride.

"Roger, be advised, someone is jamming a lot of the frequencies tonight. Try to reach Kevin, call sign four four four charlie victor. Good luck."

Wow! Aloft in a C-54, no radios, flak damage at least to the batteries, all of Europe socked in, no way to tell if he was leaking fuel, forty children aboard, nothing but a horizon, a whiskey compass and an altimeter. Once they were in the clear, no problem flying the airplane, but no way to shoot an approach. Would his fuel last until he got in the clear?

"Time for the turn to two eighty five."

No sign of the C-54.

"Fly the airplane. You have your own problems here. Keep your mind inside this plane. Kevin is good. He could fly that thing through the Pentagon if he had to."

"Starkeeper, watch out for him," he said.

Within an hour it was dark. Now they were in a sandwich of clear air between clouds below and above. The Aztec droned on, past Zurich at six thirty. John knew that his clearance did not require him to report, but he wanted information on Kevin.

"Zurich Approach, November 6322 Yankee."

"Go ahead 6322 Yankee, this is Zurich approach."

"Have you been informed about the C-54 without radios?"

"Affirmative, we believe he passed over about twenty kilometers to the south of Zurich some twenty minutes ago. A large primary return, no transponder, appeared to be on heading of two eight five. You appear to be closing with him based on what military people told us about your respective departure times off Sarajevo. Care to give a PIREP?"

"Affirmative. 6322 Yankee is a PA23-250 slash Alpha, level at ten five, ten thousand five hundred feet, three thousand four hundred meters, outside temp is two, smooth ride, between cloud layers about one thousand feet apart."

"Based on our time of passage over your station, we would report winds aloft forecast is correct. Wind at our altitude appears to be about three five knots at three two zero. How long will you stay with us Zurich?"

"Thank you, 6322 Yankee for the PIREP. We should be able to hold radio contact for another half hour."

"Thank you Zurich, let us know if anything develops with four Charlie Victor."

The autopilot checked out OK After the first fuel tank changeover, he was confident that it was operating correctly. After Zurich, the course changed to three one five degrees. Straight for England, he thought. He thought about all the allied aviators during world war two who would have flown that heading back to England. Here he was, trying the same thing, but better armed to navigate if not to fight.

"Where will we land in England," Susan asked. They had not spoken in almost an hour. It startled him.

"Gatwick. It's southwest of the center of London."

"How long?" she asked.

"Two hours, twenty minutes," he said. He reached back to hold her hand.

"How are the babies?"

"Just great, they are all asleep. I wonder if the new parents will love these children like they deserve."

"We can only trust."

"Could we stay in touch?"

"If they will let us."

"Remember the baby we took to its new home on Christmas day?

"Boy, I do. He's fourteen now."

"Where do you think Kevin is?"

"Somewhere up ahead. I hope he has enough fuel to make it to VFR. Without radios, he won't be able to shoot an approach, even ground assisted."

"Is he in a lot of danger?"

"Pretty much," said John.

"Did you ask the Starkeeper to help him?"

John turned to look at her as he answered, "Yes."

"Aerodynamics is not the only thing that holds airplanes up," he said.

"I know," she said.

They flew on in silence, watching the clouds below scroll by the wings.

Now they were on the last tanks, thirty six gallons each side. Plenty of fuel to reach England. Time for a weather report.

The met officer had given him a frequency for weather advice west of Zurich, call sign Norseman.

"Norseman radio, November 6322 Yankee on 132.45."

In ten seconds, came "November 6322 Yankee, Norseman radio, go ahead."

"6322 Yankee is northwest of Zurich at Ten five, ten thousand five hundred, landing Gatwick, could you give us current and forecast for Gatwick?"

"Roger, 6322 Yankee, Gatwick is one half mile, fog, ceiling indefinite, forecast to remain below minimums the rest of the night."

"Anyplace in England VFR or have decent ceilings, Norseman?"

"Not really, the east coast is OK, but there are not any controlled airdromes there, and no approach navaids. Say intentions."

"We will probably descend into clear air over the channel and fly VFR to a field near the east coast. Any report about my buddy in 44 Charlie Victor?"

"Nothing definite, we have a primary return ahead of you at your one o'clock, about ten miles. He appears to have slowed to maximum range speed. Everyone is on alert for them. British air force will probably scramble fighters to look for him, but the relative speed is a danger."

"Thanks Norseman, we will monitor your frequency for a while."

"Is he really that close?" said Susan.

"The man said ten miles at our one o'clock. I have turned slightly. Maybe we can catch a glimpse of him."

"What would you do if you saw him?" she asked.

"I'm thinking about it," he said.

For thirty minutes they droned on. Then, like a ghost, ahead in the gray night was the form of a four engine airplane.

"I see them," he said.

"Me too," she said.

He pushed the throttles up a bit and they continued to close up with the C-54.

In another fifteen minutes, they pulled up along its left side. Great big airplane, no lights, droning along in a murky night. Like a ghost. They flew in formation for several minutes.

John said: "Take your flash light and shine it at them. Send what I tell you. Dash is long flash and dot is short flash."

Hesitating between groups, he slowly told her to send: "Dot-dot-dot-dot then dash-dash-dash, then dot-dash-dash, then dash-dash, then dot-dot-dash, then dash-dot-dash-dot, then dot-dot-dot-dot, then dot-dot-dash-dot, then dot-dot-dash, then dot, then dot-dash-dot-dot."

They waited.

"What did you say?"

"How much fuel?

Now came a flashlight from the cockpit of the four motored C-54.

"Dash, then dot-dash-dash, then dash-dash-dash."

"What did he say?"

"Two. Must mean two hours."

"O.K. Send dot-dot-dash-dot, then dash-dash-dash, then dot-dash-dot-dot, then dot-dash-dot-dot, then dash-dash-dash, then dot-dash-dash, then dot-dot-dash, then dot-dot-dot."

"What are we sending?"

"Follow us."

In a minute, came back, dash-dash-dash, then dash-dot-dash.

"What is that?"

"He says OK."

"Wow, here we are, between layers, ten thousand five hundred feet, England socked in, a no radio C-54 beside us, but I am so glad to see them. Surely goodness and mercy..."

"What is the first call sign for England?" he asked himself. He searched the charts.

He said to her, "Watch him carefully, don't let me get any closer to him than this. Let me know if we start to."

"OK," she said. "What are you going to do?"

"Try to find a field that's VFR on the east coast of England."

"Coast watch, Coast watch, this is Aztec November 6322 Yankee." No answer.

"Coast watch, Coast watch, this is Aztec November 6322 Yankee."

"Aztec November 6322 Yankee, this is Coast watch, good evening."

"Coast watch, 6322 Yankee has a flight plan for Gatwick. However, we have spotted the C-54 off of Sarajevo that is also bound for England. We are in formation with him now. He says by Morse code that he has two hours fuel. We have approximately same fuel. We understand most of England is below minimums, any advice?"

"Stand by, 22 Yankee." One minute. Two minutes. Five minutes. Eight minutes.

"22 Yankee, we have an idea for you and your friend."

"Go ahead, Coast watch."

"We called on land line to Archbury on the east coast. They are good VFR below a thousand foot ceiling. Archbury is six miles west of the cliffs of Dover. No navigation aids nearby, but we suggest you tune 1230 on your ADF for the local radio station just south of the runway. They are presently playing a nice selection of World War Two songs due to a reunion at Archbury of Yank flyers from the war. Archbury personnel advise they will place a vehicle at each end of the runway with rotating police lights, blue lights. There are no runway lights. Field elevation is one thousand six feet MSL They report local altimeter setting is two niner niner four. Do you copy?"

"Roger, we copy all the figures you gave us, Coast watch."

"Coast watch, here is our plan. 6322 Yankee will descend over the channel to below one thousand MSL, if we break into the clear, we will lead the C-54 to Archbury. If we cannot get into the clear, we will rethink this mess and probably divert for a ground assisted approach. I can't imagine how difficult that will be for our friend, though."

"22 Yankee, Coast watch advises you clear of the French coast in two minutes. Suggest you begin your descent. "

"Roger, we will begin descent as soon as we signal Charlie Victor."

He tuned the ADF to the station given by Coast Watch. 1230 Kilohertz. Sure enough, the voices of the Andrews sisters filled their headsets. The needle pointed to 010 degrees relative. John made a course correction and blinked his running lights several times to draw attention to that fact by Kevin. He noticed the dark shape of the C-54 assume a course parallel to his.

Surely Kevin must realize that we must begin our descent soon, he thought.

"Archbury Control, Archbury Control, do you read Aztec 6322Yankee?" No response.

"Archbury Control, Archbury Control, do you read Aztec 6322Yankee?" Still a scratchy emptiness in the earphones.

He told Susan to send another Morse code message to Kevin. "Send dash-dot-dot, then dash-dash-dash, then dot-dash-dash, then dash-dot."

"What are we sending?" she asked.

"Down," he said.

In a minute, Kevin sent back, dash-dash-dash, then dash-dot-dash.

"OK, he says," John said to Susan. "Here we go."

She gave him a look and then looked out at the cloud layer below.

"Now comes the tough part," they both thought.

John reached over and for the first time in hours, pulled the throttles back a little. He trimmed for a stable descent rate of four hundred feet per minute.

In less than a minute, they and the Aztec slipped into the clouds. John could barely see the wingtips in the murk. He turned off the strobe to decrease chances of vertigo. Now the altitude was nine thousand. Water covered the windscreen. Drops flowed across the arch of the wing tops. No sight of the C54.

"That's good," he thought, "Keep that big fellow over there until we break out."

Now six thousand, airspeed one seventy knots, rate of descent four hundred per minute. Minutes pass. A few small bumps in the clouds. Now three thousand. Still no sign of clearing. Still the raindrops cover the windscreen and wing. He stole a glance at Susan. She was looking back at the babies, all still tucked in. Artificial horizon showed a rock solid descent with the bar just a quarter inch below the horizon. One dot, that's what his instructor told him. Now two thousand five hundred feet MSL. Breaks began to occur in the clouds and all at once, they were in the clear -- a dark gray ceiling above, a black sea below, but good visibility. He immediately looked to the right for the C-54. Nothing but empty gray space.

"Kevin, where are you?" he said to himself.

John descended to five hundred feet below the ceiling, level at two thousand.

"Come on Kevin, show up."

"There he is," Susan said.

Sure enough, about a thousand feet to the right, the C-54 barreled along in the night sky.

"We have about thirty miles to go, but Kevin doesn't know that. We need to send him another message."

"OK," she said, "go ahead."

"Send dash, then dot-dot-dot-dot, then dot-dot, then dot-dash-dot, then dash-dot-dash-dash, then dash-dash, then dot-dot, then dot-dash-dot-dot, then dot, then dot-dot-dot, then dash-dash-dot, then dot, then dot-dash, then dot-dash-dot, then dash-dot, then dash-dash-dash, then dot-dash, dash."

"What is it?"

"Thirty miles, gear now."

"Why so soon?"

"Someone is going to have to crank the gear down, probably. It will be slower than normal. He will need to know that the gear is down. We will have to fly up close enough to tell him it looks down."

Kevin sent his OK again.

As they droned on in the dark gray, they noticed the gear doors of the C-54 opened slowly. The nose and main gears appeared in transit, slowly moving down. It took minutes, but at last it appeared down and locked.

"Send dash-dash-dash, then dash-dot-dash. Tell him OK."

In a minute, Kevin sent, "Thanks, good luck."

"Archbury Control, Archbury Control, Aztec 6322 Yankee."

A few seconds later came, "6322 Yankee, this is Archbury Control. Say position and altitude."

"6322 Yankee is about twenty miles south east, level at two thousand."

"Good show, 22 Yankee, two thousand will clear all obstacles between you and the field. The cliffs rise vertically to about nine hundred MSL. Runway is zero four. Your flight of two is cleared to land. Police vehicles at each end of runway with blue lights. Usable length five thousand four hundred. Caution, occasional deer on runway."

"Roger, Archbury. C-54 will land first, we will make low pass to guide him to runway and then go around and land."

"Roger, 22 Yankee. Parents of students have arrived by bus from London. Adoptive parents here also. Our chaps are on lookout for you. Over."

"Roger, Archbury, ten miles now."

The white cliffs of Dover were a dark gray in the night as they swept over.

They both saw the police flashers at the same time. The C-54 had slowed and so had John. It was a blanket of black below, no lights on the ground.

Make a wide pattern, he thought, letting Kevin maneuver the C-54 around onto final. The flaps were slow to come down. John thought some poor soul in that plane was pumping a hydraulic pump as hard as he could.

Down they came toward the flashers. They had closed up now. John was just fifty feet left of Kevin's left wing tip, fifty feet above and fifty ahead. Steadily, the big C-54 came down final. Kevin got the mains on the runway about two hundred yards beyond the police flashing lights John added throttle and the Aztec rose to go around.

The runway had occasional tall grass growing between blocks of concrete. Its wheels thumped as the plane crossed each thatch. The C-54 slowed gracefully and made the turn around about five hundred feet from the end of the runway. John and Susan were already on crosswind. On downwind, they could see the C-54 roll to a stop in front of the only building on the airport. They could see the door open to a crowd of people just as they turned base.

John put the gear down and added a notch of flaps. The Aztec turned to final. They touched down smoothly and rolled out, coming down to taxi speed before they reached the C-54. They turned off the runway and rolled up to the crowd.

There was Kevin in the crowd, surrounded by happy children and parents. He looked over and saw John and Susan with the adoptive parents. It was good.

ABOUT THE AUTHOR

Starkeeper is an assembly of aviation related short stories. The first three stories involve the author's father, a flight surgeon in the United States Army Medical Corps in India during World War II. The first story is historically correct. The story about Mr. Peanut actually happened, but the names have been changed. The remaining stories, which take place in China, Burma and India during World War II and then West Virginia and Tennessee in the 1980s, are either entirely fictional or are fictionalized accounts of historical events. Identity of the Starkeeper will become clear to the reader early in the book.

The author of *Starkeeper* is John L. Hash. He was born and raised in Charleston, West Virginia and is a graduate of Duke University and West Virginia University. He is a licensed pilot and an active bulls-eye pistol competitor. He is retired in Huntington, West Virginia. *Starkeeper* is his first book. His second book, *Honey Branches: The Meade Estate* was published in early 2012.